"Any particular rea

It's a messy business for a beautiful woman.

"Don't worry. I've had plenty of practice at cutting throats and I'm very careful. I don't get a drop on me. Ever. And as for why I'm here, it's very simple. I want you to trust me."

"Well, we're off to a good start."

"I'm proving something to you. I'm proving that you can trust me. I could kill you in just a few seconds here, Mr. Ford. If I wanted to."

"I'm sure you could. What is it you want exactly?"

"Oh, c'mon now, Mr. Ford. You know what I want. I want to know where Grieves is."

She cut me then. I jerked in the rocking chair where I'd fallen asleep looking out the hotel window.

Warm blood sliding down my neck. A nasty sting from sliced flesh.

"You see how easy it would be, Mr. Ford? Now you're a federal agent, just like Grieves is a federal agent. That means you know what he knows. Am I right?"

It's never easy knowing what to say when somebody's got a razor pressed against your throat . .

Books by Ed Gorman

Cavalry Man
DOOM WEAPON
POWDER KEG
THE KILLING MACHINE

CAVALRY MAN

DOOM WEAPON

ED GORMAN

HARPER

An Imprint of HarperCollinsPublishers

This book is a work of fiction. Names, characters, places, and incidents are products of the author's imagination or are used fictitiously and are not to be construed as real. Any resemblance to actual events, locales, organizations, or persons, living or dead, is entirely coincidental.

HARPER

An Imprint of HarperCollins*Publishers*
10 East 53rd Street
New York, New York 10022-5299

Copyright © 2007 by Ed Gorman
ISBN: 978-0-06-073486-2
ISBN-10: 0-06-073486-8

First Harper paperback printing: August 2007

HarperCollins® and Harper® are registered trademarks of HarperCollins Publishers.

Printed in the United States of America

Visit Harper paperbacks on the World Wide Web at
www.harpercollins.com

10 9 8 7 6 5 4 3 2 1

To Jeremy Cesarec

CAVALRY MAN
DOOM WEAPON

Prologue

The rogue scientists Dobbs had read about always hid out in the West, though there were a few who went to South America where women were as plentiful as wine.

But now that it was 1885, now that there was transcontinental train travel, now that even small cities out West boasted the beginnings of electrical and telephone service . . . now it would be tolerable for a city man to live there. Safe for a rogue scientist like himself to live there . . .

The thing was to get away from the Army lab before anybody figured out what he was up to.

The arms merchants who had contacted him had assured him that there was nothing to worry about. They told him what to say in his retirement announcement, they told him how much money would be waiting for him out in Junction City, Colorado. They even told him how to invest the bulk of his money so he could enjoy his life no matter how much longer he lived.

But he, for his part, didn't tell them about the federal agent he'd come to know. The only one in the whole deal there he trusted.

He didn't tell them because they wouldn't like it. But

he had a sense that as soon as he handed over the materials they wanted, they'd kill him.

But they wouldn't kill him with his friend the federal investigator on hand. If anything, the investigator would kill them and then he and the scientist would have a lot of money—more money than either man had ever even dared dream of—and they would still have the materials, too. Which, as the investigator suggested, they could sell over and over again. Get the money, kill the buyer. They could probably do this four or five times before it got too dangerous.

These were some of his thoughts as he sat in his train seat looking out the window at the unfolding panorama of the West. He'd heard talk that the buffalo had been killed off but he'd sure seen plenty of buffalo in his first three days. He'd also heard talk that though the Indian wars were substantially over, there were still many fierce bands of Indians prowling the prairies, too angry to settle on reservations. But the Indians he saw from his window were disappointing as far as ferocity went. They were old and shabby and shambling, defeated people dragging themselves along the railroad tracks in search of anything the white people in the train cars might have tossed out or dropped.

He wasn't a drinker but he drank. He wasn't a brave man and every once in a while a wave of terror would overwhelm him. If anything went wrong—despite the bravado of his friend the investigator about how safe it all was—he would be in prison or dead. Hard to know which would be worse.

The drinking stilled the fear.

But no matter how much he imbibed, he couldn't silence the one word that haunted him like no other: treason.

No matter how he tried to justify it to himself, that

was what he was committing there. Even if their scheme worked and they never actually gave the plans and materials to agents of other governments, that was how any court in the United States would view what he'd done.

He had committed treason . . .

And so he drank and stared out the window at the snow-peaked mountains and the desert areas that were an alien if beautiful mauve color at dawn and at all the fuss and drama of train stops where exuberance of the new West put jubilation on nearly every face . . .

But not his.

No jubilation for a man who committed treason.

For a man like him there was just the money.

He prayed that that would be enough for him.

PART ONE

Chapter 1

The Regal Hotel
Junction City, Colorado
Room 207
12:07 a.m.
March 23, 1885

"I knew you'd wake up eventually, Mr. Ford. I put a little sleeping powder in the coffee the maid brought up."

"You seem to have a knife at my throat."

"It's dark, Mr. Ford. It's really a straight razor."

"Ah."

"My name's Molly Kincaid, in case you want to know. And if it wasn't so dark, you'd be able to see that I'm a very beautiful woman."

"Any particular reason you want to cut my throat? It's a messy business for a beautiful woman, you know."

"Don't worry. I've had plenty of practice at cutting throats and I'm very careful. I don't get a drop on me. Ever. And as for why I'm here, it's very simple. I want you to trust me."

"Well, we're off to a good start."

"I'm proving something to you. I'm proving that you

can trust me. I could kill you in just a few seconds here, Mr. Ford. If I wanted to."

"I'm sure you could. What is it you want exactly?"

"Oh, c'mon now, Mr. Ford. You know what I want. I want to know where Grieves is."

She cut me then. I jerked in the rocking chair where I'd fallen asleep looking out the hotel room window.

Warm blood sliding down my neck. A nasty sting from the sliced flesh.

"You see how easy it would be, Mr. Ford? Now, you're a federal agent just like Grieves is a federal agent. That means you know what he knows. Am I right?"

It's never easy knowing what to say when somebody's got a razor pressed against your throat.

Chapter 2

All this happened—I'm referring of course to the blade held against my throat—because an agent named Arnold Grieves had gone missing while working on a case in Junction City, Colorado. Grieves was a very good agent except for the times he got distracted by women and liquor. Then he tended to disappear, sometimes for weeks. He was a man of strong constitution where vices were concerned.

Now, I'll admit that I didn't come to Junction City in the best of moods. Something had been mentioned in a telegram about one Noah Ford going on vacation but then Grieves seemed to be lost somewhere so Ford had to forget his vacation until his fellow agent was found.

I was hoping to find him in the town and then quickly find one of those legendary mountain streams where the fish are practically suicidal.

This was my mood as I approached the City Limits sign that was mostly lost in the dirty, dank fog. What the hell ever happened to clean white fog? But this was mining country and the air was never what you'd call pure. As one silver millionaire had put it, "If you got people walkin' around coughin', you know you're makin' money."

It was the fog—as well as the rain, snow, ice, and the rain again—that had contributed to my sullen mood. I wasn't old but I wasn't young and between the rheumatism and the occasional arthritis, eight days riding in and out of mountain towns was taking its toll on my usual angelic manner.

The previous night, trying to get some sleep in a tiny cave while the snow whipped in the entrance, I even had the thought that maybe I'd give up. Just wire Washington, D.C., and the lizards who manned the desks, and tell them that I hadn't had any luck and was now heading for the beaches of California.

That was the dream, anyway, that California sun and that blue blue water. But dawn and coffee and frozen beef jerky took the dream away. Whatever else I was, I was a professional, a military investigator and a federal agent, and even though I hadn't been any good at drinking, marriage, the free enterprise system, or being a desk lizard, I was a passing fair tracker of the human being.

Now I had to see if my tracking skills could turn up an agent named Grieves.

❖

It was a mountain town, all right, Junction City, most of it fashioned hastily out of raw lumber blackened with the residue of various mining procedures, silver being the table stakes there. There were some mansions, of course; you could feel them sneer at the lowly worker houses below. The mansions were actually a bit too splendid for their own sake—minarets and captain's walks and a dormer every three feet—impressive if you didn't have any taste, like fat harlots strutting the boulevard in garish clothes.

The one odd note was that the mine was silent. Mines usually ran two, three shifts a day. Not there, I guess.

Unlike too many towns of this kind, Junction City had made the transition from a raw camp to a real town. You could tell that by the cleanliness of the streets and the general condition of the buildings. From what I'd been able to read about it, the town council held corruption to a minimum and had a very serious program for controlling the worst ravages of prostitution and gambling. You'd find them there but they were strictly controlled.

Another factor was the town council's determination to oversee the diligent pickup of garbage, fines for anyone who kept unsightly yards and that bane of many towns, the speedy collection of wild dogs.

The five straight blocks where goods were sold and money changed hands were the most imposing aspect of the place. Now, at cold hard dusk, the blocks looked like a fortress against the night itself. Oil lamps still burned in business offices; the saloons at the far eastern end of downtown poured forth the vile wonderful music of drunks and whores; and even the three church spires, normally not anything that would warm an agnostic like myself, lent me the pleasant notion that just maybe, just possibly, just hopefully, there was some kind of divine being overseeing this whole mess after all. There were three pretty fancy casinos for those who chose to spend their hours in other than churchly pursuits.

Nobody paid me much attention when I rode through the business area. Everybody was too burrowed down in their tall collars and winter coats to pay anybody else much mind. The ragged mountain winds were without mercy. The calendar said that spring had arrived. I wanted to complain to the management.

I spent half an hour registering at a hotel and hauling

my saddle and other gear up to the room. In the old days I would have traveled with three pints of rye. And the first thing I would have done inside my room was get a hot basin of water for my frozen feet and sit next to the window and watch the human parade spread out below me there on the second floor. And I would've gotten drunk in a way I couldn't on horseback. When you're riding those lonely miles by yourself you get a glow on but you don't let the liquor take you completely. It's dangerous enough out there without losing control of yourself.

I got the scalding water in the basin; I got the chair by the window and a pretty good look at all the sad human follies below—stumbling drunks; poor little kids trying to drag their fathers home from the saloons; a shotgun deputy dragging some troublemaker to jail.

The water stung and I let it sting. I'd changed into warm clothes and wrapped a blanket around me. And from downstairs an old lady brought me a cup of coffee as hot as the water for my feet.

I smoked three cigarettes, laid my head back against the rocking chair for what I thought was a rest, and didn't wake up again until I felt something cold and sharp pressing against my throat.

Chapter 3

"I can cut it a little more if you'd like me to. If I haven't made my point clearly enough, Mr. Ford."

She'd gotten a little too cute with the tough-sister talk. She was doing some pretty bad acting now.

Some facts to consider here. I'd never seen her before. I had no idea how she knew Grieves. And she was getting so carried away with her little drama, I was afraid she might cut me open just to prove to herself that she could do it.

One more thing. I was so groggy I was watching all this from a distant vantage point. I saw myself with the razor held against me. I saw the slight cut on my neck. I saw the girl's slender hand trembling with the razor. But I was so groggy, I wondered if I could actually make my move.

When I grabbed her wrist and wrested the blade from her hand, I probably squeezed a whole lot harder than I needed to. And when I came up out of my chair and shoved her away from me, I suppose I didn't have to kind of hurl her into the wall. But the hangover from the sleeping powder had left me slightly dazed and enraged.

She made a fuss out of her pain, of course. She was

now the injured party and she wanted to keep that fact well known.

The blade had flown from her hand and was now somewhere in the room. She crouched in a corner, huddled into herself. Tears gleamed on her cheeks and she made tiny grunting sounds of pain.

I went over and closed the window. That's how she'd gotten in. The wooden fire escape covered all three floors. Everything outside was frost-covered and shiny in the light of the ascending moon. Nothing looks lonelier than a small burg all shut up for the night. The only sign of life was chimney smoke from the shabby homes of the miners.

I crossed the small room to the oil lamp and turned it up. She hadn't exaggerated her good looks any. Even in a pair of gray butternuts and a rumpled black sweater, her looks had the power to startle. And startle they did. She had the formal good looks of a princess in her prime, the haughty blondness of big-city women you frequently saw on the arms of powerful men.

I tried the door. She might have somebody waiting in the hall. Nobody in the hallway. The time of the half-death as some of the Northwest Indians call sleep.

I turned back to her and said, "Stand up."

She gave up the whining and said, "You should see yourself. I wasn't kidding about how beautiful I am, was I? You should see your face."

I couldn't help myself. I had to laugh. She was so used to being flattered that she couldn't quite believe that that much time had passed without me sending compliments her way. I guess she didn't understand that since my throat still stung where she'd cut me, I wasn't in the mood for being swayed by her undeniable beauty.

I walked over to the bed, yanked my Colt from the holster hanging off the back of the straight-backed chair, and then sat down. I couldn't ever remember a conversation with a woman telling me how beautiful she was. I'd had women tell me how smart, how hard-working, how sweet they were. But never how beautiful they were.

But if anyone had bragging rights on beauty, it was this one.

"You really hurt me, Mr. Ford, you know that?"

"Who are you working for?"

"You're not going to help me up?"

"Answer my question."

"You really hurt me, the way you tossed me into the wall."

"Who're you working for?"

"I'm not working for anybody except myself and Uncle Bob."

"Who's Uncle Bob?"

"Right now I don't feel like talking anymore." She had decided to sulk. Under other ordinary circumstances her sulking probably would have been kind of erotic. Big bad man kiss away all those fake tears and then pitch her into the sack. That's where sulking usually ends up.

But hers was so obviously just one more theater turn that all it succeeded in doing was making me angrier.

"You ever had anybody stomp down on your instep?" I spoke just as my eyes contacted the straight razor beneath the bureau. I walked over and picked it up. It had black grips with small white diamond logos on each side. Not cheap, not expensive. There was a small taint of blood on the tip of it. My blood.

"They told me you were educated. Even went to college for a while. I was expecting a gentleman."

"It hurts like hell, somebody grinding down on you like that. Can hobble you up for a week."

"I'm not afraid of you."

"You will be after I stomp down on you a little while."

"I'm not who you think I am."

I wasn't sure what that was supposed to mean. I said again, "Stand up."

She put her hand out for me to take hold of and ease her to her feet.

"You don't look helpless. Now get up."

"Some gentleman."

I watched her struggle to her feet. She looked a lot cuter than I wanted her to at the moment. When she was about halfway standing, she said, "Uncle Bob!"

I had no idea what she was talking about. This was a girl who spoke in mysterious ways. I was still working on how she knew Grieves and why anybody who knew Grieves would put a straight razor to my throat.

I sensed a presence to my right and when I turned, I found out who "Uncle Bob" was.

There in the window, standing on the fire escape, was an old man in a tuxedo with a top hat who looked like every ancient duffer you see in those traveling vaudeville shows.

He tipped the hat and waggled his white-gloved fingers at the young woman.

"That's my Uncle Bob. You should let him in. He's probably freezing."

Once, a very pleasant Mexican woman with whom I'd spent a few nights convinced me to try a little peyote. I didn't use much but it had the effect of skewing my perceptions, anyway. Strange images. This was starting to feel like that peyote night again. Middle of the freezing night and some sorry old actor is in my window.

"Sure, why not let him in? He have a straight razor, too?"

"He'd never hurt a fly."

"How about a human being?"

"Well, if you won't let him in, I will."

The situation was so odd I felt I was back in my peyote dream again. A beautiful crazy girl and an ancient vaudevillian grinning and waving inside the frame of my window.

That was when it happened. There is no way to set down the feelings you have in that first moment of recognition.

There is an irritating old man in your window. He is waving like a clown and then he is not waving like a clown because the bullets from the rifle explosion you've just heard have now reached him.

The white-gloved hands spread out as the explosion lifts him up. He seems to hang in the air there a moment. Even in death the clown-likeness clings to his face. He appears to be smiling in these last moments of his life.

But his will be a spectacular end, probably the same kind of end that all those who trod the boards hope for.

Instead of falling backward, he fell forward, his top hat flying off as the tip of it touched the window. His white-gloved hands came through the window just as it was shattering from the force of his head smashing into it. Glass shards flew into the room. The girl and I turned away from them in time, though tiny bits of glass bit into our backs.

Uncle Bob continued to sail through the window. As I was to find out, he was mostly rag and bones, a tenpenny street performer who couldn't have weighed a hundred pounds. He didn't make much noise when he crashed to the floor and skidded a few feet on the broken pieces of glass his body had brought into the room.

I grabbed the lantern and turned it down. A long moment of empty wrecked window and the cold midnight air rushing in and the girl's sobs. I could hear the broken glass crunch under her as she knelt beside her uncle. "Oh, Uncle Bob, Uncle Bob."

I made my way to the window. Pressed myself to the side of it and started to peer outside. My Colt was cold in my hand as I leaned forward for a look.

And that was when the shooter pumped two more bullets at us. This time when she screamed, there was nothing theatrical about it at all.

There is always that time after unexpected violent death when most of us lose our capacity to think clearly. In war, this incapacity can get you killed. You're standing in a daze next to your friend's corpse and the enemy keeps firing away.

I pushed the girl on the bed and said, "Stay there and don't move." The bed would be safe from any more bullets.

I hunched down and went back to the window. This time I got a better look.

Oh, yes, a much better look at—nothing.

Chapter 4

According to a lot of the more misinformed magazine articles I've read from back East, there is so much violence in the West (or New West as some still persist in calling it) that Westerners are used to it. They see so much violence that they brush up against it and just move on. What're a few dead bodies more or less?

I wanted to invite anybody who still believed these hoary old tales to the hall outside my room on the night old Uncle Bob took three bullets to his back.

It was a human stampede, the sort you see when horses are in a burning barn. Pure blind panic. Pure blind fear. Pure blind screams and running this way and that. Every single one of them sure that the boogeyman who had just visited Room 207 was now about to visit their rooms, too. And with the same results.

There was no way to stop the girl from sobbing, there was no way to Lazarus-like revive Uncle Bob, so I did the only thing I could do. I took out my federal badge and walked out into the hall and addressed the mostly male group of people who stood in nightshirts and long johns a few yards from my room. Some of them had handguns, some of them had pints of whiskey. Some of them, the visionaries in the crowd, had thought to bring both.

I held up my badge and identified myself and explained that the threat was over. That I was going to be investigating what had happened in my room and that in due time the killer would be brought to justice. They knew what a crock of shit this latter point was as much as I did. The last estimate I saw from the Department of Justice said that as many as 40 percent of murderers were never found.

"You knew the man who was killed, did you?"

"That goes under the heading of the investigation. I'm sorry but right now that isn't anything I can talk about."

"There's a girl in there crying. I can hear her right now. Is she all right?"

"Physically, she's fine. But that was her uncle who was killed in there so she's pretty sad right now."

In the flickering light of the wall sconces, I saw a couple of the men tilt pint bottles of rotgut to their mouths and take a few healthy guzzles. They were calm now. And now that they were no longer afraid for their own lives, they turned into ghouls. They'd want all the details. All the blood. The smashed bone. The strange grotesque look on the dead man's face. And was there any chance—just maybe—that the girl in the room crying . . . was there any chance at all that she was naked perhaps?

A stout man in a white shirt and black trousers and wide yellow suspenders said, "It's over then, folks. You heard Mr. Ford here. It's perfectly safe to go back to your rooms. Now why don't you relax and get a good night's sleep?"

He then began moving them with the subtle skill of a sheepherder easing his flock in just before dusk.

He gently prodded each of them to their respective rooms, offered a polite good night, and when he was finished came back to me.

"Name's Kent Barlow. I'm the night man here. We didn't get a chance to meet earlier. The sheriff's on his way."

We shook hands. "You've got a way with your customers, Barlow."

"Well, first of all, credit where credit is due. You and your badge calmed them down. And my part came from sheer practice. I spent my early years working in a hotel in Brooklyn, New York. Have you ever been to Brooklyn, New York?"

"Couple times."

"Have you ever stayed in a hotel in Brooklyn, New York?"

"Stayed in Manhattan, I guess."

"Well, this shooting tonight—something like this happened four or five times a week where I was night man. Admittedly, these weren't the best hotels but they weren't too bad for Brooklyn. Shootings, stabbings, drug overdoses—never had any men killed on a fire escape, I'll give you that. But—"

"But you had plenty of practice with situations like this, is what you're saying."

"And this is the first time anything like this has happened out here. Three years I've been out here and this is the first time." Footsteps behind us. A glance over his shoulder. "Say, there's the sheriff now."

The average monthly wage for a lawman in this area of the West was around $120. He could make himself two dollars for every person he arrested if the arrest resulted in conviction.

I had a sense that this man was probably doing a mite better than that. The dark suit, the white Stetson, and the custom cordovan Texas boots plus the swagger suggested that here was a man who wouldn't settle for living on the economies most lawmen had to suffer. The white hair and cold blue eyes belonged to half the senators I'd met back in D.C.

"Sheriff Michael Terhurne, this is federal inspector Noah Ford."

His smile was as cold as his gaze. "Well, you federal folks seem to have discovered our little town."

"If you mean an agent named Grieves, that's why I'm here."

"And that's why your boys back in D.C. have been sending me a telegram a day asking if I can find him. I guess they don't have much faith in you fellas, huh? They think he's on a toot?" He winked at the night man. "He was on a couple of good ones out here, wasn't he?"

The night man looked afraid to go along. If he was as sarcastic as Terhurne, he'd make me mad. If he stayed somber, he'd make Terhurne mad.

He was smart. He excused himself and moved quickly to the stairway.

"So what happened here?"

"I'm not sure yet. Let's go in the room and I'll tell you what I know."

"What's wrong with out here?"

"You afraid of some blood, are you, Terhurne?"

"A fella could get the wrong idea about you, Ford. If he didn't know better, a fella could think you were a prick."

I smiled. "Funny, I was just thinking the same thing about you. How a fella could get confused and all."

But he wasn't finished. He thrust his hand out palm up and said, "The first thing I need to know here is are you really a federale?"

"Meaning what?"

"A badge and some papers, for starters. And tomorrow I wire D.C. to double check on you."

"They're in my room." I smiled again. "Along with all the blood."

Even a swaggering mick bastard like him couldn't conceal his distaste for blood and death.

He was able to hold his face in check when we stood in the room looking down at the mess that had once been Uncle Bob. What he couldn't control was his gulp. Big, incessant gulps followed by ragged, nervous sighs. There were a lot of men in the war like him. They just never could adjust to the carnage. I had felt sorry for them. I had my own anxieties about all the slaughter, especially in the area of nightmares. Terhurne here I didn't feel sorry for at all. I imagined all his deputies did most of the work where corpses were concerned.

A woman came in the door while I was showing Terhurne my papers and badge and pointed to Molly, who was sitting on the bed with her back to the corpse. "Mr. Barlow said to take her to an empty room. I'll stay with her."

Molly was at the point where she looked like one of those zombies you always read about in the Eastern tabloids. Creatures who are dead but don't seem to know it. She wasn't crying now, in fact she wasn't making any sound at all. Her eyes were fixed on a realm only she could see. She tripped on a small rug. The frail helpmeet steadied her and then guided her slowly out the door.

"You see the tits on that one?"

Mr. Swagger was at it again. Maybe playing manly was compensation for being such a sissy about blood.

He didn't wait for my answer.

He handed me back my badge and letter and then walked over to the rocker and sat down. His eyes scanned the corpse. It was cold as hell in there. He apparently didn't find anything interesting but he spent a good two minutes just staring at the man's head. "You know him, Ford?"

"Nope. He came in through the window. Or rather he tried. Came up the fire escape, I guess. Then he stood in the window and waved at the girl and then somebody shot him. He smashed through the window."

"What about the girl? You know her?"

"Nope. She came through the window while I was still sleeping."

"Kind of a strange story, don't you think?"

"That's not the strangest part. She fixed my drink up so I'd be asleep when she climbed through the window." I told him about the straight razor.

It seemed to grab him then. Even with the wind, the smells of death were pretty harsh.

"Let's go downstairs and get some coffee." A couple seconds after he said it, he was in the hall, waiting for me. I didn't want to give him the satisfaction of knowing I was ready to get out of this room, too. By now I'd picked the last of the glass from my back. That was the last memory I wanted to have of this place.

❖

We sat in an alcove where travelers played pinochle. Barlow brought us hot coffee. Through the doorway I could see two deputies and two men from the funeral home going up and down the stairs.

He got right to it. He didn't give a damn about the murder. All he cared about was that his name came before mine in the newspaper story. "This is my jurisdiction."

"Technically, I can take over if I need to."

He nodded his white-maned head. "Yes, that's true up to a point. But I can make your life hell if I want to."

He turned to the kid deputy who had appeared in the doorway and said, "Mr. Ford and I need to be alone here, Hayden. You know how to take care of things."

Hayden had a shitkicker grin and a pug nose and he looked harmless. "You comin' back upstairs, Uncle Mike?"

"A night for uncles, I see."

Terhurne scowled at me.

"I'm not coming back upstairs unless you screw up and force me to, Hayden."

Hayden blushed. He wore a sheepskin that looked a couple sizes too big for him. He looked like he wanted to crawl down inside and hide. "I was just askin' is all, Uncle Mike."

"You heard what I said, Hayden. Now get the hell out of here."

Hayden went away.

"He's just helping out. My regular night man has got the croup. If that meets your approval, that is."

"Uncle Bob, Uncle Mike. A lot of uncles."

He brought the mean out in me, the way some people do. I wanted to smash his asshole face in. I expected he wanted to do the same to mine.

He asked me to go over my story again but he figured out fast that I didn't have much to add. Girl awakens me says she needs help, Uncle Bob on fire escape. Three shots. Dead.

"You wouldn't try and bullshit a bullshitter, would you, Ford?"

"Not as big a bullshitter as you."

He actually smiled. "I guess I had that coming. I mean it's some story. If you weren't a federal man as you say you are, I'd half expect you did in Uncle Bob yourself."

"I ran downstairs into the alley and shot him and then ran back upstairs so I could get glass in my back."

"You got glass in your back?"

"You want to see it? Molly got some, too."

"She's got one fine pair on her."

"Yeah, you said that."

"You thinkin' she's kinda beholden to you?"

"I'm thinkin' I came here to find Grieves. Or find out what happened to him, anyway. And I'm thinkin' that Molly knows something about him. And I'm thinkin' that maybe if I find out who killed Uncle Bob I can find out where Grieves is." I drank some coffee. He watched me. He definitely wanted to do some work on my face, too. I set my coffee down. "What you're thinking is that for whatever reason, you want all the glory in this."

I started rolling a cigarette. I waited for him to say it. I had to give him some help. "So what do you want, Sheriff?"

"Me? Hell, I just want to clean up this murder is all."

"I'm sure you do. But that's not the only thing you want. The way I've been insulting you, most lawmen would have tried to shoot me by now. But not you. That means you're willing to put up with my guff because you want something."

He leaned back in his chair. He was one of those men who could swagger sitting down. "You're no dummy."

"Thanks for the compliment. Now let's talk about what's really on your mind."

He leaned forward, stared right at me. "I've got my pride."

"That doesn't come as a shock."

He sighed and leaned back. "Like I say, I've got my pride. And I'm not used to askin' people favors. Not around here, I'm not."

He produced, from deep in the pocket of his suit coat a half-pint of bourbon. He took a long and reverent drink. He made a face when the alcohol hit his belly. But at least he didn't shudder. I wondered how much he drank while on duty.

He shoved the bottle over to me. I shoved it back.

"We got an election comin' up here. And to be honest I'm not as popular as I used to be. I'm expecting somebody to run against me. And that would be the first time that ever happened."

"And if you solve a murder like this one, you'll look good again."

"I know I can be a little arrogant sometimes." He smiled. "That comes from havin' too much good whiskey and too much good tail in my life. Man like me, he gets to believing he's maybe a little better than everybody else. And that can turn people against him."

"I guess you didn't hear me, Terhune. All I care about is finding Grieves. I have a feeling that means finding out who killed Uncle Bob tonight. And that's all I care about. I don't have to worry about getting votes. Those are all yours."

❁

Barlow showed me a room where I could sleep for the night, a room without any corpses.

"You ever see the girl before tonight?" I asked him once we were inside.

"No, can't say that I have."

"How about her uncle?"

"Nope. Him, neither. But remember I'm the night man. They may have come around during the day."

The next question had to be stated diplomatically. "The sheriff seems like a decent enough fella."

This was, of course, a statement, hinting that he might not be a decent fella at all.

He frowned. "I'm taking it that as a federal man, you're asking me a question in confidence."

"I am."

"Because if my opinion ever got out—Well, I have to live here. I like my job, the pay's good and—"

"I won't repeat anything you say."

I went over and sat in the rocking chair, leaving him standing by the door.

"And this is just my opinion, of course."

"Of course, Mr. Barlow. Just tell me what you want to say."

He was still nervous. "Well, there are some who think the sheriff is a little too friendly with the rich people in this town."

"Meaning he does them favors that he wouldn't do for other people."

He smiled. "Well, you can't blame him. I can't, anyway. I'm the same way. You like it when the important people pay special attention to you. As they do sometimes."

"You sneak them in the back way late at night?"

He laughed. "I could write a book about how many important men sneak out late at night and meet girls in our rooms on the second floor."

He was starting to wander. "You think the sheriff has ever covered up a crime for anybody?"

"Not a serious crime. Not a robbery or arson or—"

"—murder?"

He shrugged. "Not that I know of."

"You ever give the sheriff a room late at night?"

He laughed. "The sheriff's just like a twenty-year-old buck when it comes to women. He can't get enough of them. And those are the kind of men he hires, too."

"You ever run into a man named Grieves?"

This time the smile was broad. "He'd be hard to miss."

"Oh?"

"I know he's supposed to be missing—and I assume you're out here to find him—but I'm sure he's sleeping off a bad drunk somewhere in one of the nearby towns."

"He drinks a lot?"

"Drinks and parties. He was like a cowhand at the end of a trail drive. He couldn't get his hands on enough liquor *or* enough girls. You should've seen him. He sure didn't worry about money or what people thought of him. You'd think a federal man would be a little more worried about his reputation."

I had to agree with that last statement. Given the unpopularity of federal men, people enjoy sending angry letters to the agency back in Washington detailing all the many ways that a particular federal man had upset/humiliated/debased the citizens of their town. Sometimes the agency takes it seriously, sometimes not. Depends on what the federal man's being accused of.

"Well, I appreciate you talking to me about Terhurne. And you don't have to worry about me keeping it secret."

He started to turn to the door and open it but then he stopped. He frowned again and said, "You'll meet a man named Swarthout and a woman named Ella Coltrane. They're the two richest people in town. Or were, anyway, before the silver in the mine started running out."

I remembered that the mine had been shut down when I got here. No second or third shift.

"Anything special I should know about them?"

"Well, first of all, they're the sort of rich people who give rich people a bad name. A lot of wealthy folks treat folks like us with some respect—but not those two. Anyway, they both spent a lot of time with Grieves. I couldn't tell you why. But either Swarthout was showing him the town or Grieves was out at Ella Coltrane's. She's a fine-looking woman. If I wasn't married—"

I laughed. "A hotel man who doesn't believe in a little something on the side?"

"Not me. I've got a wife and three kids and they're my life. From the things I've seen, you cheat once or twice and then you slowly start cheating a lot. It's like a contagion or something. It just starts taking over your life."

He left a minute later. I got out of my clothes and into bed. I rolled myself a cigarette and lay there listening to the night sounds. There was comfort in those sounds. Sometimes I'd be on treks as long as a month when I barely saw two or three people a week. Some fugitives chose to hide out in the mountains or the deep forest and I had to go after them.

But the birds and the raccoons and even the occasional bear had become like kin to me over the years. There was a sweetness and innocence in them that you only seldom found in human beings. I'd said this once to somebody—that I often preferred the company of animals to the company of people—and she gave me a very strange look. I suppose I would've given myself a strange look, too.

Right before I slept, I thought of Molly. She knew something, something dangerous to her, dangerous as it had been to her Uncle Bob. But would she be willing to tell Terhurne or me what it was before it was too late?

Chapter 5

In the morning, I ate a big breakfast at a restaurant where at least some of the town's elite chose to eat. You could tell they were important by the derbies, cravats, walking sticks, and sizable rings they wore. They ate at two long tables near the back. This was to separate them from the trash like me and the modest merchants and shop employees who ate much humbler breakfasts and hurried on their way.

The waitress said, "In case you want to know, that blond one is the mayor, the one with the Vandyke beard is the richest banker in town, and the lady with them is Ella Coltrane, who inherited a short-haul railroad that mostly does business with the mine."

I flipped her the gold piece I'd promised if she told me about who the highborns were. She caught it and grinned. She had one of those big amiable faces that most successful eateries have at least one of.

"And here's one for free. The banker, Nels Swarthout, and Her Highness Mrs. Ella Coltrane also own the mine. But they're going to close it in a few months because the silver's running out. A lot of the miners want to strike so that Swarthout and Ella can't get the rest of the silver out—and then leave the miners with no jobs at all. And by the way, Swarthout is the worst tipper in town. Cheap cheap cheap just like a birdie."

I'd figured that those three had to be special. They didn't even eat at the long tables.

"Who usually sits in the empty chair?"

"That'd be Sheriff Terhurne, whenever he can make it."

"He's probably busy."

She winked at me. "He's probably busy all right." She used her wet rag to clean up some tobacco that had fallen from the smoke I'd rolled earlier. "From the description of that girl he's got over in his jail, I'd say he found himself a witness and maybe a special friend."

"Why would you say that?"

She laughed. "Terhurne has a sweet tooth where the ladies are concerned. So do the other men he's around. May be catchin' up with him, though. He may not get himself reelected."

A man at the next table called her over. I piled tobacco into some cigarette paper and lighted up. Cigars seemed to be the preferred smoke in the back half of the place. Expensive cigars.

Despite all the commotion the previous night, I'd slept well. I felt rested. Washington had supplied me with the name of the boarding house where Grieves had stayed briefly and a visit to his landlady was my next stop. Grieves had been trying to bust up a counterfeiting organization rumored to be working out of town here. He'd kept in close touch with D.C., most of the time by telegraph. And then suddenly—nothing.

His wife, my last wire had told me, was barely holding on. She was six months pregnant.

As I stood up, I got that uncomfortable feeling that I was being watched. Not casually, the way you happen to notice somebody in your peripheral vision. But examined, studied.

When I got my hat on, I turned and saw that it was the blessed trinity—the banker, the railroad owner, and the mayor—who'd been looking me over. They didn't smile or nod or offer any sort of recognition at all. But they weren't apologetic about studying me, either. They just kept on looking. The mayor leaned in and said something to the young woman. She and the banker nodded somberly.

They relaxed and went back to their conversation.

I had the feeling they weren't going to invite me to a party any time soon.

"Looks like you got yourself some new friends," the waitress said as she passed by my table again.

I walked alongside her to the front of the restaurant. The crowd was thinning some. There was a line at the cash register. The people in it looked like they were in a hurry. "I wouldn't bet any money on that."

"You know something? I wouldn't, either. You be careful. Those three sure don't look happy to see you."

❁

The landlady turned out to be a landlord.

"People expect me to be a woman just 'cause I run this place," the sprightly little gent in the coonskin cap told me. The cap didn't exactly blend with his work shirt and work trousers but it probably made him happy. "And I'm a real man, too, don't think I ain't. Fought in three different Indian wars. Got three wounds and I can show 'em to you if you'd like to see them."

"Maybe I can come back some other time to see them. Right now I'm here to get any information I can."

He smiled with a pair of storeboughts that looked to be too big for his small mouth. "I was just givin' you shit. The missus died five years ago, right after I retired from the railroad. So I took over runnin' the house here. I just like to rag people a bit because they's always expectin' a woman."

We stood on the sunny wraparound porch of a massive two-story house that was relatively new and extremely well kept.

"I put my heart and soul into this place. I do it just like the missus did it. She worked night and day on this place, believe me." His voice got raspy. "She's still here with me, far as I'm concerned. I talk to her all the time, even if people say I'm crazy." He grinned through the tears in his voice. "Hell, people said I was crazy before she died. So I might as well go on bein' crazy now."

And lonely, I thought. But I wasn't here as a social worker.

"I really need to talk about Grieves, Mr. Chester."

"Oh, yes, Grieves. He was federal."

"Like me."

"Say, that's right. Just like you."

"Did you get to know him at all well?"

He thought a moment, his gaze wandering to his front lawn. "He only stayed here a few nights. He took up with Swarthout out to the mansion—the one Swarthout can't seem to unload on anybody." He made a face. "Those're Sidney's turds."

I was beginning to wonder if he might be crazy—truly crazy—after all.

"Sidney's turds. Out on the lawn there. Sidney's never supposed to come over here on my lawn. We got that agreement. Sidney ate one of our little kittens. I woulda killed him but Old Man Sourbreigh give me his word that Sidney wouldn't never come on our lawn again. He even built a fence for him in his backyard. But look at those turds. They got yellow streaks in 'em. I can see the yellow streaks from here." He raised his gaze to meet mine. "That's the sure sign that they belong to Sidney, the yellow streaks. I'll have to go over there and climb all over Old Man Sourbreigh, which I kinda hate to do because he's one hundred and three this spring. But them is definitely Sidney's turds."

"Yeah, I know. With the yellow streaks."

And then, as if a switch had been flipped up, he came back to reality. "Your Mr. Grieves. The federal man?"

"Uh-huh?"

"Was gone most of the time. Didn't even take his meals here much and didn't know what he was missin', either. I got this Mexican cook Carlotta, you ain't et till you et her food. Then he snapped his fingers. "Say, he took off to that mansion so fast he left some stuff behind. I bet you'd probably like to see it. I put it all in a sack. You know he never did come back to get it."

We went inside. The vestibule had a stained-glass section above the door, a clawed coatrack, a small table for mail. The house smelled of pipe tobacco, furniture polish, and the various plants held in a variety of vase styles.

We climbed a long staircase with new runners. At the top lay a line of doors for the roomers. A door stood open on a bathroom. A man with shaving cream on his face stuck his head out and waved his straight razor at us. Straight razors I could do without for the time being. "Mornin'," he said.

"Mornin', Mr. Phibes. This here's a federal man. Friend of Grieves."

"Sure wish they'd find him," Phibes said. "Played cards with him a couple of times. Pretty sure he cheated me."

He laughed hoarsely. "The way I figure it, he owes me twenty dollars."

We went into a room near the bathroom. "Ain't been able to rent it since Grieves went missing."

A pleasant little room with a single bed, a three-drawer bureau, an easy chair set next to the lace-curtained window that looked out on a large backyard. There was a crucifix, a small framed painting of President Lincoln, and a calendar all on the west wall. On top of a small table was a stack of magazines. Some of them looked to be several years old. There were three yellowbacks.

"I put it right here in the top drawer," Chester said. "And there she is." He said this as he pulled the drawer open and reached inside. A moment later he handed over a cloth sack that couldn't have weighed more than a pound or two.

I didn't bother looking inside. That would come later.

"Well, I'm goin' over to see Old Sourbreigh. I'll walk you downstairs."

"I appreciate the help, Mr. Chester."

"All my pleasure, Mr. Ford." Then he laughed. "I hope you find Grieves and I hope I find Sidney 'cause that's one dog who's gonna get a whuppin', believe you me. You can't play croquet when you got dog turds all over the yard now, can you?"

"No," I said, "especially when they've got yellow streaks in them."

Chapter 6

There was a kind of battered nobility in the face, the busted nose, the scarred right cheek, the missing tooth and the way the shabby work clothes gave the massive body the touch a sculptor would.

He came right up to me on the street and jabbed a finger at me and said, "I want to talk to you."

I wasn't afraid of him but I wasn't eager to piss him off, either. Those hands of his could reduce bricks to dust.

"I get to know your name before you start telling me what an asshole I am?"

He didn't smile. But then I hadn't expected him to. "My name's McGivern. Will McGivern. I do the bargaining for the miners here. Only reason I ain't in the mines is because I have to go to court and stick up for one of my men Swarthout's tryin' to railroad into prison. All Sam done was go back into the main office to get his lunch pail. Swarthout walked in on him and claimed he was trying to steal stuff. Hell, only reason Sam was in there is because earlier in the day he'd asked Swarthout about getting a couple days' advance on his pay so he could send one of his kids to Denver for this here hospital. Kid's coughin' up blood."

Most people, politicians excepted of course, don't talk in this kind of bawling, nonstop verbal assault. Either they run out of breath first or they pause out of consideration to polite society. You know, they let you ask a question or two here or there.

All of this was interesting enough as information but I wasn't sure of what it had to do with me.

"You're a federal man. You could tell Swarthout to let Sam go and drop the charges."

Any time you attach the word "federal" to a name, that name, to a lot of people, takes on the aura of power. Then you find yourself in the position of disappointing them. And disappointing yourself. Most of the people who come up to you are asking for well-deserved help. Only rarely can you help them. And when you tell them that local officials have more power than you in most cases, their faces go gray. You know about local officials being corrupt or indifferent.

And that's how I was going to look to Will McGivern as we stood in the middle of the street, passersby watching us as if a fight was going to break out. I got the sense that McGivern was associated with fights breaking out.

"I'm sorry, Mr. McGivern, I don't have any jurisdiction in something like this. I'm an investigator."

"Yeah, some damn investigator." The smashed-up face scowled. "I tell you about a little kid who's coughin' up his guts and all you can say is you don't have no jurisdiction here. Then who does? Last year, five men died in that mine up on the hill and we still ain't seen anybody from the mining department."

"I need to be going now, Mr. McGivern. I'm sorry about the kid and Sam." There was no more to say, sad as it was.

"You ain't no better than that last one out here. I seen

him all drunked up and carrying on while me'n the men was bustin' our humps in the mines. Then I run across him way outside of town tearin' up the land and scarin' the hell out of all the animals. You federal people stink. He wasn't worth a damn and neither are you."

He was shouting again and jabbing the air with his finger. Then he just turned and stalked off toward the courthouse. So much grief and rage in him and it hung on the air for a long time. I just stood there and rolled myself a smoke.

And then somebody came up and said: "That man's poison. You're well shut of him. He's also dangerous."

I turned and there was the one and only Mr. Swarthout, banker and mine owner.

"Next you'll tell me he's a socialist," I said.

"Oh, he's a lot worse than a socialist. He's an out-and-out communist."

He was a dapper one, he was, and the way he spoke you knew he was never challenged. Or, on the odd occasion when he was, he resorted to using that most efficient and legal of weapons, gossip.

"He says you've got a miner on trial for something he didn't do."

"If you mean Sam Wells, Mr. Ford, the men know they are never under any conditions to enter the main office unless they see me or one of my employees in there. I make that clear to every one of them the day they start. And despite what he claims to the contrary, I'm sure he was in there stealing something."

"His kid sounds pretty sick."

He looked right at me and said, "I'm sorry for that, Mr. Ford. But if I go easy on Sam they'll start taking advantage of me every chance they get. Rules are rules."

Yes, I thought, rules are rules. Unless you're rich enough to ignore them.

"Good day, Mr. Ford," he said and walked off in his expensive city suit.

❖

I spent the next two hours doing the kind of work the Pinkerton boys and girls do. I went to the post office, I went to a church (Grieves was a Methodist and so a Methodist church it was), I went to all three barbershops, I went to a haberdashery, and I went to the livery.

I wanted to see if Grieves had established any kind of pattern while living in Junction City. The post office remembered him and said that he got very few letters and that he tended to talk up his role as a federal man. The minister said that he had heard of Grieves but had never met him. The barber in the second shop I visited told me, reluctantly, that Grieves liked to get his hair trimmed every few days and that he always smelled of fresh whiskey when he stopped in. The barber also told me that Grieves spent just about all his time in the chair asking questions about the pretty ladies who passed by the shop window. The barber said that this irked some of his customers because Grieves obviously didn't care if a woman was married or not, he obviously considered all women fair game. The haberdasher had no problem speaking right up—Grieves was a loud, irritating braggart who had nothing but disdain for this man's goods. "I buy 'em straight outta Chicago. They're not good enough straight outta Chicago? He made sure he insulted my little shop every time he came in here."

I picked up my only useful piece of information inadvertently in the gunsmith's shop where a man named Randisi checked the trigger mechanism on my Colt and while doing so said, "You're the federal man."

I said I was.

"You seem a lot tamer than the other one. That Mr. Grieves."

"He come in here, did he?"

Randisi, a nice-looking gentleman of fifty or so years, smiled and said, "Oh, he came in here, all right. Mostly to tell me that I didn't know my business and that he couldn't find a single firearm that he'd be willing to buy, unless I'd take Confederate money."

Grieves continued to make friends.

"But he did buy one .45 from me."

"Sounds like he thought he was doing you a favor."

Randisi laughed. "It wasn't for him. He made that very clear. He said that I'd set aside an old Navy Colt for a friend of his and that the friend forgot to pick it up before he left town."

"You remember the man's name?"

"Sorry. Just his initials. N.D. The man wouldn't give me his name. Kind of a secretive fella."

A gun for a friend. Sounded wrong but I wasn't sure why.

"One other thing."

"Oh?"

"He was in a hurry. Said he was on his way out of town."

"He wouldn't have been nice enough to tell you where he was going by any chance, would he?"

Randisi laughed. "He wasn't nice about anything, Mr. Ford. Not anything at all."

Chapter 7

Grieves had slept his first two nights in a hotel a block from mine. The price was 40 percent more per room per night and had a much more decorous layout, including a formal dining room where an aggrieved husband had thrown a drink in Grieves's face one night.

I learned this by canvassing all four of the town's hotels. I even spent a few minutes in the YMCA on the off-chance that he'd exercised there. But between the women and the whiskey there probably hadn't been much time for anything else.

A fine representative of the federal government. From what I'd known about him, he'd always enjoyed his vices, as most of us do, but he kept them quiet. But for some reason, when he hit Junction City, he'd gone a bit crazy.

The incident with the angry husband naturally interested me. The so-called concierge—who seemed to double as the desk clerk—was a narrow man with eyes too large for his skeletal face. He wore a dark suit that gave him a funereal touch, even though I was sure he thought he was being awfully Continental.

"We're just not used to that sort of thing here at the Imperial," he said. "We get a much higher order of clientele than the other hotels do and they tend to settle any of their arguments in a gentlemanly fashion."

He was as full of shit as a madam on the witness stand but his information was useful. Or at least interesting.

"I take it the other man was a guest here."

"One of our favorite guests. A brother of the territorial governor."

"I take it Grieves wasn't one of your favorites."

"He was here for two nights and if he'd tried to make it three, we would have had to ask him to leave." Then: "And his friend was even more obnoxious."

"His friend?"

"I personally never saw the man. I work strictly days because I'm also the concierge." He'd mentioned this three times already. "But his friend—and right in the dining room—vomited into a flower pot."

I tried not to smile.

He glared at me.

"We just don't tolerate that sort of thing."

"Do you have a description of the man?"

"As I said, I work during the day. Fortunately, I never had to lay eyes on him."

"Do you know what the argument was about?"

He went into a spell of finger-snapping that would make a flamenco dancer proud. A workman pushing a large box on a cart was apparently giving the concierge great and abiding displeasure.

"You don't bring anything like that through the front door, young man. What sort of place do you think this is?"

The man looked eager to tell him exactly what sort of place he thought this was but then he tempered his zeal and said, "Around back?"

"Of course around back. Good Lord."

When the offense went away, I said, "I asked you if you knew what the argument had been about."

"Your man Grieves seemed to think he had the right to ask a married woman to accompany him up to his room. Naturally, Mr. Soames took umbrage at that sort of vulgarity. He told Grieves what he thought of him and then sat back down at his table. But Grieves wouldn't leave him alone. He forgot about the woman and just started in on Mr. Soames. He called him so many vile names and so loudly that some of the older women got up and left. Grieves wasn't easy to handle. We had all three of our bellhops trying to drag him out of here."

"Was his friend still with him?"

"Of course. Luckily, he was passed out by this time."

"How did it end up?"

He offered me a chilly smile. "Your Mr. Grieves did us the favor of passing out, too. The bellhops carried him out of here as if he was a corpse."

"And you think it ended there? Grieves didn't come after Soames later or vice-versa?"

"We got Grieves up to his room along with his friend and one of our bellhops stayed outside the room with a handgun. In the morning, both Mr. Soames and Grieves checked out within half an hour of each other. Thank God there wasn't any more trouble."

Grieves had just kept right on making friends.

Chapter 8

I was just approaching the sheriff's office when I heard angry voices coming from the alley ahead.

The woman's voice was especially sharp, sad, and angry. I walked to the alley. A rangy man was listening to a small and very pretty woman who was jabbing her finger up at his face, giving him an explosive lecture.

Then she slapped him. You could see that his instinct was to strike her back. That was the uncivilized man in him. But the civilized man took over. His body slumped a bit. Resignation. Then he noticed me.

I just passed on and went inside the office.

I went to the stove and grabbed the coffeepot and poured myself a big hot cup of the stuff.

"Is Molly Kincaid still here?" I asked the deputy. I showed him my badge. "I'd like to talk to her."

"I just shouldn't let you do that." This was the kid deputy from the previous night. He looked small behind the large span of front desk in the sheriff's front office.

"You don't have any choice. I'm federal."

"Yeah but federal's Washington, D.C., mister. And to tell you the truth, I couldn't locate that on a map even if I had an hour. But the sheriff, he's right here in town, so if I was to let you go back in that cell and talk to that gal—well, my uncle'll be here a lot sooner than some telegram from Washington tellin' me I got to do what you say for me to do."

That was when the man I'd seen in the alley came in. He was probably in his late twenties with a stern, intelligent face, tall, lean, purposeful inside his jacket woven of Indian-blanket material. His cheeks colored when he saw me.

"Are you helping this man, Hayden?"

"Can't help him, Knut. Don't have permission to help him."

Knut put out his hand. "Knut Jagland. I'm the first deputy. Can I help you with something?"

I wondered if I'd have gotten the same smooth treatment if I hadn't witnessed the embarrassing scene in the alley.

I showed him my badge.

"You're the federal man. Sure. How can I help you, Mr. Ford?"

"Noah'll do fine. I'd like to see Molly Kincaid, is how you can help me."

"Well, of course." He nodded to Hayden. "Hayden didn't mean to be unhelpful. He's a good young man. He just needs to get permission from either the sheriff or me for anything he thinks is important."

"That's all I meant, Mr. Ford," Hayden said.

"That's fine, Hayden. And I'm Noah. To everybody, all right?" There's enough tension between federal and local that any time you can climb down off your high horse it's helpful.

"How come she's being held here, anyway?"

Knut shrugged. "Won't cooperate. Won't explain a darn thing to the sheriff or me. Says she has her reasons.

And so far she won't budge. She doesn't seem to mind jail all that much."

"She gets good food brung over from the café," Hayden said. "Meat, potatoes, vegetable, and a slice of pie. Nothin' wrong with that now, is there?"

"You hold things down here, Hayden. Noah and I are going back to the cells."

"Don't expect much activity this time of day," Hayden said.

"Help yourself to some more coffee, Noah," Knut said. "I'll bring a cup for Molly."

I looked around the office while I waited for him to get a cup.

It was more modern than I would have expected. Posters explaining the laws most people were curious about. A four-drawer wooden file cabinet where attorneys-at-law could search for back arrest records. A wall of well-organized WANTED posters divided into violent and nonviolent criminals. And four comfortable-looking chairs for visitors. The floor was clean, the walls had so recently been painted a light blue that the paint smell remained faintly on the air, and there were three spittoons for those so inclined.

On the way back to the cell, Knut stopped and spoke quickly and softly: "Sorry you had to see that, Noah. Every once in a while I spend a little too much playing poker. I never win. I don't know why I think I will. But I always go back. This time I lost a lot of money. My wife figured that out when she got up this morning and came down here to tell me about it." He touched a hand to his right jaw. Forced a smile. "She's got one hell of a right hand."

"It's your business, Knut. Not mine." I smiled to put him at ease. "I've argued with a few ladies in my time, too."

His raw-boned face grinned, making him look five years younger. "That little wife of mine is nobody to mess with, believe me."

Molly was sleeping when we got to her cell but she woke up at the sound of the key being inserted in the lock. The beauty was still there but it was blanched. Somebody had contributed a change of clothes—another heavy sweater and a different pair of butternuts, these green—and her blond hair was mussed in most places. Still, when she looked up at me as I came into the cell, the princess shone through it all. Be damned tough to take all her looks away.

On the floor next to her cot was a Bible that she grabbed after sitting up. She put it on her lap.

Knut gave her the tin cup of coffee.

"Coffee," she said. "I appreciate it."

Knut said, "I'll be leaving you two alone."

"You see anything of that attorney man?" she said.

"Not yet. He should be along. I know he was in court with the sheriff this morning."

He nodded to me, stepped out of the cell, locked it up. There were four small cells in a small back room. The floors were clean and for all the closeness the chamber pots didn't smell much at all. The other cells were empty. There was only one window and it was barred. It sat high up and to the right of the back door.

Molly took a big drink of coffee and said, "I've been in worse places, case that's what you're thinking."

"I was actually thinking that this isn't too bad for a jail."

"Oh, yes, only the most elite criminals stay here. I believe the queen of England was here not long ago."

"Did she bring her maid?"

Molly smiled. That smile could do permanent damage if you were of a romantic nature.

"Why, Mr. Ford, don't be silly. She never goes anywhere without her maid."

I sat on a three-legged stool and drank my coffee. "You got yourself a lawyer?"

"He's kind of cute in a stupid way."

"Well, that's the first thing you always look for in a lawyer. Cute."

"Better than ugly."

"You got me there."

"I wish everybody was attractive. Wouldn't that be a sweet world then? Everywhere you look, everybody looks like they just stepped out of a storybook."

"He helping you at all? Your lawyer?"

"He can't help me."

"Why?"

"Because I won't let him help me. I don't want him to help me."

"In other words, you're still not cooperating with the sheriff."

"The sheriff has a fancy for me."

"I imagine a lot of men have a fancy for you."

"How about you? Do you have a fancy for me?"

"I suspect you know the answer to that already, Molly. It'd be hard not to have a fancy for you."

We fell into a silence. Way up front somebody came in the door. A conversation started up.

"You know you could walk out of here any time you wanted."

"I know."

"They're not holding you for any reason except not cooperating."

"I don't plan to cooperate, Noah."

"Why not?"

She leaned back against the cell. The green eyes were elegant in the gritty sconce light of the cell block. The odd thing was that she now looked both younger and older. Just one more puzzling thing about this lost young woman.

"You know how I said I wish everybody looked like somebody out of a storybook?"

"Yep. You just said it a couple of minutes ago."

"You're pulling my leg but I'm serious."

"So you're not cooperating because you want everybody to look like somebody out of a storybook?"

Anger. "You're such a shit. I shouldn't even be talking to you."

She sat up abruptly, spilling a trace of coffee on her dark sweater. She daubed at it with long slim fingers. "Well, thanks a lot. I wouldn't have done that if you hadn't been such a shit."

Just then—just a flash—something I could see without quite putting a name to—I saw a hint of her true nature. The one behind the playfulness and the bravado. Rage and a sense of persecution. A sense of deep resentment, so deep that it seemed crazed to me.

"How old were you when you had sex the first time?" she demanded of me.

"That's a hell of a question."

"Come on, you shit. Tell me."

"Fifteen, I guess."

"Well, you want to know how old I was?"

The rage was escalating fast.

But I didn't want to know. Right now it was the last thing I wanted to know.

"I was eight. Eight years old, goddammit. And he was a minister and I didn't stop bleeding for days. And he probably would've kept on doing it except his wife walked in one time. And you know what she did? She had me put in a home for crazy people. So nobody would believe me if I told them what the minister had done. I stayed there for two years. And you know what, you filthy piece of shit? The man who ran the place did the same thing to me the minister did."

There were no tears. Just that anger. At me, at the men who'd violated her, and maybe most especially at herself.

"Now, you get out of here. I heard my lawyer come in up front there and he's the only one I'm going to talk to. And I'm not going to tell him anything, either. Because me and Uncle Bob, we figured out a way to get our dream. Where we'd have everything we needed. And now that he isn't here, I'm going to have the dream all for myself."

No warning. Her coffee cup, mostly dregs, flying across the shadowy space between us, banging off my forehead.

I suppose she expected anger. I suppose I expected anger. But all I did was lean down and pick up the empty cup and say, "Somebody killed your uncle because of what you won't talk about, Molly. That means that they're going to try and kill you, too. I'm sorry for all that happened to you. I'm sorry it hurt you so much and made you tough. And you are tough, Molly. But you're not tough the way this killer is. You're not tough that way at all. Let either me or the sheriff help you before it's too late."

"Oh, sure," she said. "And I bet I know just how you'd 'help me,' too. Now get the hell out of here."

I yelled for a key and then I turned back to her and said, "We're not all like those men, Molly. We're really not."

Somehow Grieves had seemed more tolerable back in St. Louis.

Dobbs now realized that this was because Grieves

had no choice but to be tolerable. He wanted what Dobbs alone possessed.

But when the two men met in the weary cold winds of Junction City, and after the money had changed hands, and after they'd fired their bellies with the best saloon whiskey they could find in such a burg—then the real Grieves emerged. And Dobbs found him obnoxious, a loud and boastful man who physically and verbally abused anybody he didn't care for and who constantly flashed his federal badge as a way of intimidating people.

But, as poor little Dobbs found out on the second day of their time together, Grieves was far more than merely obnoxious.

The two of them had been out on the plains for most of the morning. Every quarter mile or so, Grieves would see something he wanted to blow up with the new grenades Dobbs had created in the munitions lab. For all his size and bluster, Grieves was like an evil, spoiled child. He seemed to get an almost sexual thrill out of watching trees, old barns, deserted and rotted wagon beds, even gravestones, destroyed in the smoky hellish fire of destruction.

The gravestones were especially bad. Dobbs spent fifteen minutes trying to talk Grieves out of blowing them up. Didn't Grieves have any conscience? Dobbs asked him angrily. These gravestones were the sacred emblems of lives lived and now passed. These gravestones signified the splendid memories the living held of the dead. These gravestones—and here Dobbs had pointed directly at two of them—guarded the bodies of infants who'd died at less than six months old.

You can't just blow them up, Grieves. They're not yours to destroy. Leave them alone, Grieves. Please. Please, Grieves.

But of course he blew them up, chunks of stone like daggers flying through the air, the grass around the gravestones suddenly on fire.

All Dobbs could think of was the two little girls whose gravestones had been destroyed. And how their folks would feel when they went up there next time and found the stones reduced to rubble.

But that was just the first terrible shock Grieves had in store for the timid Dobbs.

The next one, later on, would haunt Dobbs the rest of his life.

Chapter 9

For my noon meal, I decided to eat where the workingmen did. I hoped the place would be quiet enough so that I could look through the sack of Grieves's things I'd picked up at the boardinghouse.

Nothing made any sense yet as far as Grieves went. He hadn't filed any complaints via telegram. The handful of people I'd talked to about him hadn't reported him seeming unduly upset about anything. He'd kept up correspondence with his wife. D.C. had told me that she'd received word from him just before he seemed to have vanished. And he'd lived the way he'd always liked to live, in the constant presence of women and liquor.

I passed a dress shop that was obviously for whatever passed as the carriage trade in Junction City. The dresses cost a lot more than most women could afford to pay even once in their lives. Through the window I saw a woman looking at me. A very pretty, dark-haired woman dressed in a lacy frock that emphasized the slender but well-appointed body. The dark eyes watched me curiously, showing no emotion. It took me a bit to recognize Ella Coltrane, the woman who owned the short-haul railroad. She'd be shopping there, of course.

She surprised me by gathering up her shawl around

her shoulders and coming up to the front door. "You're Mr. Ford, aren't you?"

"Yes, I am."

"Would you like some company?"

"Sure. But I doubt you'll want to go where I'm headed."

She hurried out. Joined me on the walk.

"Fine day, Mr. Ford."

"Fine day."

And it was a fine day. Clouds like the sails of schooners riding a wind so pure it took you back to your childhood. Even the temperature was cooperating.

We walked. Her skin was fair and freckled, her dark eyes vivacious. She was in her late twenties. She had the kind of intelligence that could amuse you or abuse you at will.

"Do you even know who I am, Mr. Ford?"

"Sort of."

"That means they told you my name and that I'm rich and that I'm a widow."

"The widow part I hadn't heard."

"Cholera. A rafting trip. Four of them dead in a day. Including my brother."

"I'm sorry."

"They used to call me dirty names, this town. Now they feel sorry for me. I don't know which is worse."

"There are probably worse problems."

She slid her arm through mine. I had no idea what she wanted. I was sure that when I found out I'd feel a lot less flattered by her attention.

"So where are you headed that I wouldn't want to go?"

"I saw a little café. The Cup and Saucer."

"Oh, my God, take out life insurance before you go in there."

"The food that bad?"

"Not just the food. The miners. All they do is get drunk and complain about what a bad deal they're getting."

"It's not a life I'd want."

She stopped, withdrew her arm from mine. Then she turned and said, "You're not a communist, are you?"

"Nope, not at all."

"A socialist?"

"If you mean should the workingman get a fair deal, then I s'pose I am a bit of a socialist. Right now they're the only ones fighting for the common man. The government sure isn't."

"But you're the government."

"I like to think I'm helping the average man. Not hurting him."

"So that means you throw in with miners?"

I scratched the back of my head. "I guess it does."

She didn't try to hide her anger. "Well, you're sure not the man Mr. Grieves is. He's much more intelligent."

"You know Grieves?"

"I've enjoyed his company on two or three occasions."

"Well, then I'd like to ask you some questions."

"Why don't you go ask your miner friends some questions?"

And she hurried away.

The Cup and Saucer didn't want for decorations. DON'T LET HIM CHEAT US ANYMORE signs had been nailed to the walls every few inches.

I found an empty corner with a wobbly table and two chairs. Tobacco smoke was as heavy as fog in some places. The air was raw with the stench of bloody meat frying. The man who took my order had the busted nose of a drunken brawler or a former boxer. The atmosphere was saved only by the strong slant of sunlight streaming through the soiled windows.

For the first twenty minutes or so, alone with my coffee and cigarette, I was able to concentrate on the sack with Grieves's things in it.

Most of it was irrelevant to my investigation. A comb, a handkerchief, a yellowback, change, a letter from his wife telling him how much she missed him and how lonely the nights were now that her pregnancy was in full bloom, and assorted buttons, cravat clips, pens, and a pair of telegrams from D.C. inquiring about his progress on the counterfeiting ring he was trying to locate.

I almost closed the sack up until I realized that stuck into the same envelope as his wife's letter was another piece of paper.

I opened it up and found it to be a list of some kind.

> Nathan Dobbs
> The convent
> The mansion

Next to each was a penciled check mark indicating, I assumed, that he had dealt with this person or place for whatever reason.

Nathan Dobbs sounded familiar. I wasn't sure why. But I knew it was a name of some prominence and significance. But why? It didn't have anything to do with counterfeiting. That I was sure of. Why had Grieves listed it here? Then I remembered the initials N.D. from the gunsmith's.

For a time my mind was relieved of trying to figure out what the list meant.

The talk among the miners was getting loud, an anger giving the din a sharp edge. I didn't pay much attention, but I was forced to pay attention when a large bald man was knocked into my table with a fist the size of a boulder. He was even angrier than McGivern, the miner I'd met earlier.

The bald man tried to right himself but couldn't. Seeing the inevitable, I grabbed my coffee cup, stood up, and walked backward into the wall. The man continued downward, striking the table and knocking the legs out before he crashed on top of it to the floor. His head struck my boot. The crashing sound seemed to hang there for a long time.

The even bigger large man who had put him down them lunged forward, maybe to kick him. Four other miners grabbed him, restrained him.

The man who'd waited on me, and who was apparently the owner, rushed into the melee. He had a club. But not for long. He was shouting for the fight to break up and swinging the club over his head. But one of the men grabbed it from his hand and punched him right in the face. His nose became a red geyser of blood. He covered his face and fell back into a chair.

This was the sort of situation the mine owners could exploit, the arguments among the men themselves. If the owners put out a newspaper they'd splash something like this all over the front page: MINERS FIGHT EACH OTHER IN CAFÉ—DISAGREEMENT IN THE RANKS. Then they'd identify the dissenters, the ones who didn't want to strike, and they'd go after them with bribe money to keep the dissent going. If all else failed, they'd move in their goons, Pinkertons, or freelance thugs. They were everywhere these days. Owners paid top dollar for thugs.

As the man on the floor started to grapple at air and

pull himself up, his opponent said, "You're the only one what can convince them other miners to strike, Lou. He wants to get all the silver out of there he can and then run out on us. Maybe if we don't dig that silver for him, he'll think things over. We got to stick together, Lou. We got to strike."

The semicircle of miners in dusty, soiled work clothes raised busted hands in solidarity. They wore the kind of dirt that didn't come off. Some of them looked like raccoons, the weariness and mine dust encircling their deep-set eyes. The rich people who own mines are the most ruthless bosses since the heyday of slave owners. Over in Pennsylvania and down in Kentucky they had five-year-olds working the mines for ten cents a day. The little ones could wiggle into the most dangerous places of all. Never mind that they missed school, developed black lung by ages eight and nine, and were frequently crushed to death in those wiggle places they were sent into. Satan was happy, as were his rich followers.

"If we go on strike," said the man on the floor, grabbing on to a chair and pulling himself up, "then we all starve. Better that a few of us work and share whatever food and oil we can afford to buy."

There was as much sorrow as anger in these men. They had wives and kids to support. There couldn't be anything worse than watching the ones you love starve and go sick on you. It cut your manliness right down the middle.

The mine whistle.

The clarion call to keep the rich richer.

They trudged off. The man who'd been knocked down joined them. The one who'd hit him clapped him on the back. "We ought not to be fightin' each other, Lou. Don't you see that's what they want us to do?"

Lunch pails banged against legs. Heavy work shoes tromped the floor. They filed through the door then as a unit, throwaway men laden with grief and fear.

Unions were slowly taking hold in the West. The battles were brutal. The rich hired Pinkertons and thugs of all stripes to penetrate groups of workers and report back everything they learned. In Wyoming, twelve railroad workers had been cut down in a gun battle with hired goons. The workers probably would have stood a better chance if they'd had weapons.

I sat there for a time finishing up my coffee. I was now the only customer. The owner with the bloody nose came over.

"You're lucky you didn't get hit." He still pressed a rag to his nose.

"I try to avoid that whenever I can."

"You can afford to be a wiseacre. You don't got this bloody nose."

I decided he might be a good source of information. "There a convent around here?"

"You mean for Sisters and things?"

"Yeah, for Sisters and things."

"Well, I guess then we'd be talking up in the hills. It ain't exactly a convent. It's more like a refuge. They help run the little hospital here and teach at the school for Catholics but they stay at the place up in the hills. Them Sisters did all the work themselves, too."

I wrote down the instructions he gave me.

The nose started bleeding in earnest again. "I wonder if I broke something. I kinda agree with them boys. I mean, mine owners are real bastards. I came out here from Pennsylvania. They worked my old man to death and half the time he had to fight to get his wages. The pricks. He died coughin' blood up so bad we had to keep a bucket by his bed."

Then he waved me off. He went away to do something about his geyser.

A sweet warm afternoon was a good time for a ride in the foothills. Maybe the nuns would make a better man of me. A lot of people had tried.

Chapter 10

The convent was a half mile out of town, built of logs and perched on a hill surrounded by pines. Below it stretched the farmland that the Sisters and their helpers tended in the warm months. Behind the convent I could see a white barn, a small corral for the horses, and a separate area for six dairy cows.

Not too long ago this would all have been timberland. But whoever had homesteaded it—and it might well have been nuns—would have had to fight and conquer the land as they would any other foe. Cabins would have been built first, then outbuildings. Crops would have been planted right away. Wells would have been dug soon, too. I hadn't seen any water nearby.

There was a tranquility in that place that I let myself enjoy. It was as if the cabin and its land were within some kind of protective bubble. The air was sweeter, somehow. One time in the war I'd holed up in a monastery. I'd been wounded in the leg. The two monks who'd resided there had been killed in a crossfire. I'd patched myself up as well as I could and then set to eating anything I could find that didn't need fire. Why invite the enemy in? I apparently hadn't done a great job working on myself. An infection set in and I sweated a day and a half through delirium. But when I woke up it was odd—although I didn't have much strength, I felt a peace I don't think I'd ever known, not even as a boy. I hid out there another two days until I was sure I could travel well and fight if I had to. The trouble was that as soon as I left the monastery that feeling of serenity left me. I was then just one more grizzled soldier cast out of paradise.

I could hear the nuns praying inside. The whipping wind probably stifled my knock.

I'd been expecting a nun in a religious habit of some kind. This was a willowy middle-aged woman in a seaman's sweater and a pair of dungarees cinched with a very female belt. Her good Irish looks were just beginning to fade along with the chestnut color of her hair.

"Morning, may I help you?"

"Sister, is it?"

"Sister Jane, yes."

I introduced myself.

"How may I help you, Mr. Ford?"

"Do you know anything about a woman named Molly and her Uncle Bob?"

She turned back to the three women seated at a long table beneath a huge wooden crucifix. "It's about Molly." To me, "They've been staying here a while. Is there some trouble?"

"Well, right now she's in jail, I'm afraid."

"Molly is in jail?"

"And I'm afraid that's not the worst of it. Somebody murdered Uncle Bob."

"Good Lord." She was obviously shaken. The other nuns had heard, too. She stood back so I could come inside.

One half of the long room was as neatly organized as a military barracks. Two sets of bunk beds, a kitchen area, a tall bookcase packed with books, and three long poles suspended by wire from the ceiling that sufficed as a closet.

In the center of the cabin was a grotto of sorts. The enormous crucifix, a wooden kneeler, a framed painting of the Virgin standing atop a globe, and a small incense dish, the smell of the stuff sweet on the air.

The table was the sort used for picnics, with benches on both sides. I was introduced to the three other nuns, each dressed in street clothes, and handed a cup of steaming coffee. I sat on a stool at the far end of the table.

All of the women looked sensible and capable. No fluttery butterflies here. On the other hand, they'd kept themselves female. I'd seen mountain women who looked as burly and tough as their menfolk.

Tin plates and tin cups sat in front of everybody. I'd been given a green glass cup. Visitors only, I suspected.

They looked at me politely but with the kind of fearful curiosity you see on the faces of people who are hearing terrible news.

"How did this happen to Uncle Bob? He was such a vulnerable old man."

While I gave them the particulars, Sister Jane's eyes filled with tears.

"And why is Molly in jail? She didn't kill her uncle."

I explained that Molly wasn't being cooperative and Terhurne had chosen to hold her in jail.

"Right now, I'm trying to find out something about Molly's background. Did either she or her uncle tell you much about themselves?"

"Just that they were going to be rich and build us a convent that would put all other convents to shame." This from the white-haired nun. She smiled and not without fondness. "That was from Uncle Bob, of course. He was quite the dreamer."

"Did he say how he planned to get rich?"

"One night," said the red-haired nun, "he told me that there was a man who was going to help him get rich."

"Did he say who the man was?"

Sister Jane said, "Grieves was a name he mentioned."

"How about Molly? Did she ever say they were going to be rich?"

"Oh, yes, and we were all going to live in a fairy-story world. She really believed that, I think. Both that such a world existed and that she'd live in it one day." She laughed. "Uncle Bob, on the other hand, was more practical, his dreams I mean. They were both going to build us a fine big convent but while Molly was off living in her fairytale world, he was going to go to 'Frisco' as he called it and have himself a good time."

A nun who looked to be part-Mexican said: "He always said that he was too polite to tell us exactly what a 'good time' meant. Though he did say he'd be goin' to confession a lot."

"But you can't remember anything he said about how he was coming into all this money?"

The white-haired nun said, "He was always very vague about that, even when he was drinking."

"I take it he drank a lot?"

"Not as much as he wanted to—"

"Once or twice when Molly let him have some whiskey from this flask she kept from him—"

"It didn't take much for him to get very merry—"

"I don't know if you've noticed that, Mr. Ford, about men who drink a lot. They can drink a long time but it doesn't actually take very much to get them drunk."

This was a freewheeling moment when everybody was pitching in thoughts and it ended when Sister Jane said: "He just kept saying Grieves and another man were going to make him rich. But he'd never tell us who the other man was. He kept it a real big secret. It was kind of cute, the way he made such a big deal out of it." She paused. "This was when he wasn't telling other kinds of stories about taking us to Europe and fixing up our school and telling us how he was personal friends with all kinds of important people. He always talked so big and most of the time it was a lot of fun. But every once in a while Molly couldn't take it anymore. Then she'd smile and say, 'Oh, c'mon, Uncle Bob, that's just another one of your whoppers.' And he could tell some big ones."

"According to him," the red-haired nun said, "he'd pretty much fought the Indian wars all by himself. And he'd been asked by President Lincoln to be his personal bodyguard for a time."

"He knew we knew it was all bosh," said the white-haired nun. "But that's what made it fun for us and for him. He was actually just a tent performer who had very bad bones. He said that he'd made his living for a long time doing a little dancing and singing a few songs and then telling what he called his life story. He claimed to have saved a lot of people in his time."

Sister Jane said, "One story had him saving Molly from a burning orphanage. And another story had him saving her from going over a falls after her father suffered a heart attack and died in the canoe."

"And don't forget when he saved her from the bear," said the red-headed nun.

They were like gleeful young girls. A visitor had come and so they had an excuse to please him and themselves.

"So, you see, Mr. Ford, you can pretty much take your pick. A burning orphanage, a canoe going over the falls, or a bear about to attack a girl." Sister Jane touched long fingers to her cheek. "I suppose we sound cruel to you, Mr. Ford, as if we're making fun of him. But we all loved nights around the convent listening to his tales."

"He was the most fun we've had in years," said the white-haired nun. "And Molly was a saint. She put in as many hours around here as we did."

"Where did they sleep?"

"There used to be six of us. There's a small shed with a stove in it. Room for four more. Meals and everything else they took up here."

Sister Jane said, "Do you think any of this had to do with Uncle Bob's murder?"

"That's the part I'm not sure of. That's what I'm trying to find out."

An alarm clock opened up with enough clamor to wake up every living thing within a quarter-mile radius of the place.

"Our meal time is over," Sister Jane explained.

"We give ourselves exactly twenty-two minutes, the full thirty minutes for supper." The white-haired woman dabbed at her mouth with her white cloth napkin. "It's easy to forget we're nuns sometimes out here on our own. So we stick to a very regimented life."

"Sister Jane thinks she's a drill sergeant," said the red-haired one.

The other two nodded in agreement.

"Imagine how they talk about me when I'm out of the room," Sister Jane said. Then: "We all had our little fun at Uncle Bob's expense. But now let's bow our heads and pray for him. And that Molly gets out of jail right away."

I thought that was the prayer.

I was wrong. Prayer meant prayers plural. Our Father, Hail Mary, Glory Be. My wife had been Catholic. These were familiar sounds.

A few minutes after the prayers were finished, the nuns headed to the hooks next to the door where their coats were hung. They shrugged into them and we all went outside.

"Since they were staying here, Sister Jane, I suppose they left some things behind."

"The shed is right around back. You can see for yourself." I noticed her blue eyes gleaming. "I'm never as strong as I need to be. It's just so sad, the two of them. She can still turn her life around. And Bob was a good man. I suspect he lived most of his life outside the law, as they say. But deep down I think there was a decent man there. If you saw him with animals, you'd know what I mean. They loved him."

She caught my smile.

"I don't suppose that means anything to you but I've found that animals have a pretty good sense of human beings. They seem to know the kind ones and go to them. And they shy away from the mean ones. Not always but often enough that they're pretty reliable about who's a good person and who's not."

We had walked around back of the house. What she had referred to as a "shed" was a replica of their log cabin, only half as large. "We try to keep it up. There are always people needing somewhere to sleep."

"And eat."

One of the nuns had mounted a horse and was riding toward timber; another was working on a wagon that had been turned on its side, something wrong with its axle apparently; and the third nun was busy setting up wood to be chopped into firewood.

She put out her hand. We shook.

"We'll be praying for you. We don't believe in execution but we do believe that murderers should be in prison for life."

Then she set off for the small barn that housed the livestock.

❂

The interior of the cabin was smartly set up. A clean oilcloth covered the floor, the walls were lined with newspapers that had been glazed to be more attractive. A kitchen area, two comfortable-looking beds with heavy red quilts, and potted plants set here and there. A lot of frontier people would have considered this shed a pretty enviable place.

Molly and Uncle Bob had moved in. On the counter in the kitchen area were a few framed photographs of the two of them taken a few years earlier. Molly looked to be about fifteen, Uncle Bob looked pretty much the same. There were a couple of Molly's report cards from the sixth grade with straight A's. On the back of one a teacher who signed herself Nadine Pentecost commended the young girl for "poise, charm and general intelligence. She is especially endowed with a passion for theatrical readings, which she gifted us with many times."

Uncle Bob had a collection of odds and ends that spoke to a life of travel and pleasure. Stubs attesting to his visits to amusement parks, baseball stadiums, and various museums, musicales, and tent show performances everywhere. He'd obviously spent some time in the East because he had brochures depicting beautiful young singers across a span of years. I thought of what Sister Jane had said about animals recognizing good souls.

Molly's bed was easy to spot. A large doll with a tiara

sat atop her pillow. The tiara was missing most of its sparkle.

Because there was no dresser or bureau of drawers, I looked in the other place people choose to put their valuables. I leaned down and felt around underneath her bed and found a wooden box.

I opened the lid. Newspaper clippings, magazine articles, ribbons won as prizes, locks of hair, odds and ends of cheap jewelry—a jumble of memories, all of them seeming to be innocent until—

Four books for small children. Each of them with drawings of beautiful princesses and knights and castles in the air. They were cheap books and badly illustrated. That made me feel sorry for Molly. She should have had better editions. But even those crudely drawn books were enough to inspire her. That was where Molly really lived. She was such a young woman of parts—violent enough to put a razor to my throat, innocent enough to dote on fairy tales, strong enough to tell the law she wouldn't cooperate.

I thought about buying her a gift. She'd be in need of something sweet and unexpected after all that had happened. Of course, I was also hoping that my little gift might start her to talking, too.

❁

Back in town, I rode my horse to the livery and then started off to the newspaper. I barely got out of the barn the livery used before the owner, a swarthy man with a massive head and dark eyes that never looked pleased with anything they saw, said: "I hear you been askin' about Grieves."

I turned around. Of course.

"Yes, I have. Do you know him?"

"I don't. But my daughter does. She stayed out half the night at a party in town here and when she got home, you can bet I tanned her hide good."

This sounded sloppy even for Grieves. Being with a young girl was a pretty bad problem to have, especially in a strange town.

I was almost afraid to hear the answer: "How old's your daughter?"

"Twenty-one."

It was almost like a joke.

"Well, that's of legal age."

"It ain't when she lives under my roof. Boyfriend of hers, no good little bastard, he run off with somebody else and left Lulu Jane with nobody to marry. So she's still at home and by God she'll live by my rules."

"Did she tell you anything about Grieves?"

"Just that he was real drunk and got in a pretty bad fistfight with some real small man who came in late. She's seen plenty of fights growing up with her brothers but she said this fight was really something."

"She know the man's name?"

"Didn't say. Just said they acted like they really hated each other."

"Any chance I could talk to your daughter?"

He nodded. "She's right down the street at the Thrift Shop. She's got a good job there, especially since she started running the mail-order-bride service."

I thanked him and walked down the street. The day was still warm and comfortable. Just about everybody around looked to be in a pretty good mood. Spring has got a power no other season can claim.

Lulu Jane turned out to be a rangy young woman with dark hair and a pretty if somewhat pinched face. All I could see of her clothing was a white blouse and a red vest. She stood behind a tall counter surrounded by a store where secondhand clothes of every description packed the place. Unfortunately, they had the smell of secondhand clothes. But that wouldn't keep poor families from buying everything they could there.

"You here about a bride?" she said. "I just got a new catalog in and I'll tell you these are some of the prettiest gals you'll see outside of Paris, France."

She reached down. I was about to see this fabled catalog.

"Well, actually, I was here to see you, Lulu Jane. Your dad said it'd be all right if I came over here and talked to you." I showed her my badge.

Her cheeks blazed instantly. "He said it'd be 'all right' if you talked to me? Shouldn't I be the one to make that decision?"

She didn't wait for an answer.

"I'm twenty-one years old. I don't need his permission for anything. I'm saving up money for a room here in town and then it's goodbye to him."

Is there anything more pleasant to get dragged into than a family squabble? There's something about arguing with blood kin that makes people insane.

"Well, I guess I'll leave all that up to you, Lulu Jane. What I wanted to ask you about was a man named Grieves."

She smiled, looking even prettier. "He makes it mighty tempting to move to a big city. Not with him, I mean. But just to a big city in general. All the new fashions and the parties and the interesting people. If my mail-order-bride business wasn't doing so good here, I'd give it some serious consideration." Then she looked at me as if really seeing me for the first time: "How come you're asking about Mr. Grieves?"

"Your dad said he got into a fight with somebody one night when you were there."

"Oh, he sure did. He always keeps saying he just wants to have a party that lasts forever and that's what it was sort of like. There wasn't anything shameful going on. Everybody was a little tipsy was all. But then this little fella comes in and they go into this other room and right away you can hear them yellin' at each other. And then all of a sudden they start into this fistfight. The little fella wasn't any match for Mr. Grieves, that's for sure."

"Did you ever find out what they were arguing about?"

She thought a moment, biting her lower lip as she considered my question. "Well, it was something to do with business because Mr. Grieves said, 'We're partners and you're not gonna back out now.' "

"Did you happen to catch the man's name?"

She laughed. She had a sweet girly laugh. "Well, as I told you, everybody was a little tipsy and that was me included. About all I remember was that it started with a 'D', I think. And maybe that's not right. But it could be."

"So you didn't hear any more than that?"

She blushed. "Not that I can remember." Then: "I know Mr. Grieves has disappeared somewhere. I just hope he's all right." Then: "I'm sure my dad told you how I was left behind by Vern Tiller, who ran off with somebody else. Well, I don't mind telling you that I've been pining over him for more than a year. And Mr. Grieves's party was the first time I just let go and had fun and didn't think of Vern, not even once. Well, maybe once. But no more than that. I sure hope Mr. Grieves comes back."

She smiled. "And invites me to another one of his parties."

The gravestones weren't enough. Not for a man of Grieves's destructive appetites. As day was pushing on dusk, that sad shadowy twilight time that always reminded Dobbs of the family he'd left behind, Grieves suddenly pulled his horse up short and said, "Give me one of those grenades."

"What for?"

Grieves looked genuinely shocked. "What for? You're askin' me what for, you little bastard? Because they're mine, that's what for."

"Haven't you destroyed enough things for the day?"

"You still sulkin' about those headstones? You're worse than a woman, Dobbs. I'm goin' to take you to a party tonight that's gonna make a man of you for sure. You wait and see. Now you drop down and get one of those grenades and you bring it over here, you understand?"

No use arguing. For all his fancy ways, Grieves was not of the human species. Dobbs had met a few military men like Grieves. No conscience, no restraint. Evil, self-ish, self-absorbed little children. Why in God's name had Dobbs ever thrown in with him?

Dobbs carefully carried the grenade to Grieves. So far not one of them had misfired, something he'd not yet had to mention to the federal man. Though Dobbs had told him that these grenades never exploded in the hand of the man throwing one of them, this grenade, for all its power, was just as risky as all the grenades that had come before it. Three soldiers had been killed in the trials leading up to Dobbs pronouncing his inven-tion completed. The Army hadn't cared. If it had one entirely expendable asset, it was the foot soldier.

Dobbs stood in the chilly half-light, squinting a bit now, trying to figure out where Grieves was going. All he could see was Grieves walking slowly across a wide patch of buffalo grass. The patch was empty except for an unsaddled horse that was enjoying the taste of the grass.

There was nothing for Grieves to blow up there.

And then, thank God for the half-light so he couldn't see it clearly, Dobbs watched in disbelief as Grieves readied the grenade and then lobbed it right at the horse.

Dobbs had never seen such carnage before. And he would never forget it. No amount of willpower, no amount of whiskey, no amount of saloon whores could ever put the sight out of his mind. The horse's head was ripped from the body and flew several bloody, brain-spilling feet into the air. And from the hole where head was separated from body gushed an unthinkable rain of blood as the horse collapsed to the grass.

"Did you see that, Dobbs? Did you see that?"

The evil child, delighted.

Dobbs swung around backward and vomited as he had never vomited before.

Chapter 11

Liz Thayer, who I'd been told ran the newspaper, was about five two and ninety pounds at the most. Blond hair pulled back and tied into a bouncy tail. Big brown eyes that would have been sweet if they didn't look anxious. Faint wrinkles at her mouth and eyes. They looked good and true on her. White blouse, a man's ancient brown cardigan sweater, and a pair of brown butternuts that showed off her very elegant little behind.

When I walked in she was standing on a stool and thumbtacking flyers to a cork board. The flyers appeared to be samples of the quality of printing you could get there. Few newspapers survived without being a job printer as well.

She looked down at me.

"Be right with you."

"No hurry."

"You're the federal man?" She said this while stretching and talking around a mouthful of thumbtacks.

"Aren't you afraid you'll swallow those?"

"You didn't answer my question."

"Well, you didn't answer mine."

"Well, as all the six-year-olds say, I asked you first."

"Yes, I'm the federal man. How many tacks do you have in your teeth?"

"They're not tacks, they're long nails about three times as long as tacks."

"They look like tacks."

"That's because they have bigger heads. And I only have two of them between my teeth." At which point she held up a new poster, picked a nail from between her teeth without relinquishing the hammer, and nailed the poster into place. She did the final one in half the time. Then she turned and jumped down from the stool.

She walked over to the counter, set the hammer down, dug in the left pocket of her butternuts, pulled out a small handful of nails, and laid them down next to the hammerhead.

"Coffee?"

"You people drink a lot of coffee."

"You may not have noticed but it's pretty cold here sometimes. But I should warn you, my granddad says, and I quote, 'Liz makes coffee that tastes like goat piss.' "

I laughed. "You two like each other?"

She went behind the counter and poured herself some coffee. "Depends on the month, day, hour, and minute. It's a constantly shifting relationship."

"I've had a couple of those."

"I have, too. Unfortunately, I was married in one of them. He was wise enough to walk away from it. I mooned for a long time. Are you familiar with mooning, Mr. Ford?"

"Much more than I care to be."

"Good. At least we understand each other about the important things."

She came over and leaned on her side of the counter. The longer you looked, the more you liked. Behind her I could see the Standard Washington Hand Press and the type forms, the key elements in the laborious business of printing. In the East I'd seen a linotype machine, the wave of the future they'd said, where setting the type was done in hot metal and set in long strings of words. This cut the biggest chore of printing—setting type by hand—in half. Out here, with few able to afford it, the linotype was the stuff of legend.

"So go ahead and ask me another question so I can get back to work. And quit staring at me because it makes me nervous. For one thing, you're too old for me."

I blushed. That's the true sign of manliness—to blush when an attractive lady digs at you a little.

Then she said: "Damn. I'm sorry. It's just I hate men so much—"

"You're right. I am too old for you."

"Yeah, but you're sayin' it nice and I meant it mean."

"I'll probably survive."

She touched my hand, which I had resting on the counter. I liked the feel of her much more than I cared to at the moment.

"Maybe we'd better just stick to business."

"Good idea. I want to know about a federal agent named Grieves."

"You mean the 'heartbreaker'?"

"As in ladies' man?"

She shrugged. "I suppose to some women he was. Not to me."

"You ever talk to him?"

She thought a moment. "Just that one time, I guess. He wanted to borrow a couple of back issues."

"Do you happen to remember what they were?"

"No. But I can find out. We charge a penny to take

out a back issue and you have to sign for it the way you do at the library. The issues he took'll be listed on the checkout card. I can't do it right now, though."

"Durn right, she can't," said the stubby little man with the oily apron. He worked the press with a certain passion that bordered on violence. "Right now I need her to set some lines of type for me."

"You going to let me say goodbye at least to the gentleman, Tom?"

He grinned. "Depends on how long it takes."

"Tom," she said in a perfectly droll voice, "is under the impression that he's boss of this newspaper. And you know something? He may just be right."

❀

He'd probably been the joke of his schoolhouse. Skinny, sort of bug-eyed, and already balding, even though he couldn't have been much more than twenty-two or -three. He wore a cheap brown suit that looked too big for him and carried a briefcase that was so swollen it looked to be half his weight.

He came right at me. He put his hand out to shake when he was still five feet away.

Before he reached me, a woman in a bonnet and shawl hurried up to him. They had a conference right then and there. Five, six, seven minutes or so. Very intense. I couldn't hear the words. The wind whipped them away. Finally, she waggled a finger at him and said, "And I don't expect to get no bill from you till you get this settled in my favor. Some lawyer you are."

She stalked off.

"Friend of yours?" I said.

He smiled. "Just one of the local lunatics. If we had a day or two, I could explain what she wants me to do. Since I don't have any important connections here, they think they can walk right up to me and I'll help them. The ones who really need help, I don't mind. But a lot of them are like jailhouse lawyers. They get in an argument with somebody about property rights or something like that and want me to sue them for a lot of money." Then: "You're the federal man and I'm David Longsworth. I heard about Molly Kincaid. She needs legal advice."

We stood about ten yards from the sheriff's office. The late afternoon traffic was getting heavy. People heading home, some probably with mighty long journeys.

"I met that agent of yours one day. Didn't like him."

"Why's that?"

"Way he treated me. I know I sort of look like a short version of Ichabod Crane but he kept rubbing it in. Calling me 'sonny.' "

"What'd you talk about?"

He snorted. "Wanted to know how much money the widow Coltrane was worth."

"Ella Coltrane?"

"One and the same. I told him I didn't have any idea. Everything she and Swarthout have is in the mine."

"Wonder why he wanted to know."

"Same thing I wondered." He lifted his briefcase. A faint expression of strain played across his face. "Well, wish me luck with Molly Kincaid. I don't see how Terhurne can hold her much longer."

"I hope not. She's had a rough time of it."

He smiled. "You've restored my faith in federal men. Sure glad they're not all like Grieves."

Chapter 12

I had two messages waiting for me at the telegraph office. One was from D.C. The boss was informing me that he'd gotten word that several foreign agents who operated out of the capital had been sniffing around people in our office for information about Grieves. He said that Grieves had apparently put his name in the foreign-agent circuit indicating that he was ready to do business and that he had something that every agent would want to bid on. The boss said that this information had come to a German agent via a telegram from Grieves dated six days earlier. But that apparently none of the foreign agents had heard from him since.

Every major capital in the world had spies thick as fireflies on a hot summer night. The agents seemed to have special powers for sensing that certain classified information or weapons were on the contraband market. They were rarely violent, they didn't have to be. The men and women selling the secrets were greedy for money. They were only too happy to deliver the goods without any fuss.

But I wondered if this particular set of agents mentioned in the telegram weren't out of luck. By the time they'd figured out where Grieves had been, the matter would have been closed. At least I hoped so.

The second telegram was from Grieves's wife. "You are the only hope my children and myself have of finding my beloved husband and their father. As you know, I am expecting another baby, too. I'm praying for you every waking moment."

I felt like a shit. She was back at home well into her pregnancy worried that her "beloved" husband might have suffered an accident or something. I didn't want to be the one to tell her the truth. That, I would happily leave to somebody else. I'd file my final report and that would be that.

Rogue agents weren't all that uncommon. A fair number of temptations were put in our paths, everything from woman flesh to real gold. And just about everybody was susceptible at one time or another. The number of rogue agents was a lot higher than our government liked to let on. It wasn't any different from the way police departments covered up rogue cops. A few years back in Chicago more than seven hundred cops had been fired at the same time for being crooked. As one of the local newspapers had pointed out, given the pool from which the cops were drawn, a good number of the new officers would be just as corrupt.

I stood at the table in the telegraph office trying to figure out how to respond to Mrs. Grieves. What I came up with was:

    I HAVE LEADS I AM FOLLOWING.
    HOPE TO HAVE GOOD NEWS SOON.

I knew it was a chickenshit telegram but didn't the woman deserve at least a sliver of hope? The "beloved"

Grieves was probably in some whorehouse at that moment. His wife deserved some pleasure, too. A little false optimism was all I had to offer.

❖

I took a chance on Swarthout not seeing me in his bank. He seemed to be out on the street a lot. Or maybe he'd be in a meeting. If he found out what I wanted, he'd ask me a lot of questions I didn't want to answer.

The bank clerk was a young man straight out of a Horatio Alger novel, those yellowbacks that always featured young men who rose from humble circumstances to become scions of industry. His celluloid collar was so tight you could see the red marks on his neck. He'd battened down his cowlick with axle grease.

"My pleasure to serve you, sir. Good morning!"

"I need to speak to an assistant manager."

"Perhaps I could help you, sir."

"Sorry. Say, is Mr. Swarthout in?"

"Sir, Mr. Swarthout is out on one of his community calls. He makes a point of locating people in need and helping them. We're very proud of him."

I wanted to add a few red marks of my own to the kid's neck. I believe the word is strangulation.

"Then please find me the assistant manager."

"May I say what your business is about?"

"Just say it's federal business."

An invisible fist punched the kid in the belly. "Federal? Say, that is something."

He went away and came back with a beleaguered-looking man with a weak handshake and dog-sad brown eyes.

"Norm said 'federal' business, sir?"

I showed him my identification.

"Maybe you should come back when Mr. Swarthout is here, sir."

He hadn't even asked me what my business was.

"Afraid I'm in a hurry. Is there somewhere we could talk?"

I was adding to the sadness in his dog eyes and I didn't feel good about it. I imagined that Swarthout was probably an imperious boss and would work this poor little bastard over pretty good for talking to a federal man.

With great resignation, as if he knew that the noose was about to be placed around his neck, he said: "Very well, sir. Very well. Let's step into my office."

As he slipped behind his desk, he said, "Philip Axminster is my name. Guess I should've introduced myself out there. But I'm nervous about this. Nobody divulges any sort of information—other than the routine things, I mean—without Mr. Swarthout's approval."

"I'm told he used to run slave ships."

"I beg your pardon?" He'd been startled.

"That was a little joke."

"I apologize. I'm just a little anxious about this." Then, in a childlike voice, after an enormous gulp, "Am I in any position to refuse answering questions?"

I was tempted to make a joke—try to calm the miserable little man down—but I didn't seem able to amuse him.

"I'm only going to ask you one question. And, yes, much as I hate to say it, you can refuse to answer until either Swarthout is here or you have a lawyer present."

"I sound like an old stick-in-the-mud, don't I?"

"You sound like a man who probably has a wife and children and needs to worry about keeping his job."

He smiled nervously. "You're very polite for a federal man. And I appreciate it."

"If you're talking about Mr. Grieves, that's who I'd like to talk about."

"Oh, dear."

"What?"

He thought a moment. "It's just—well, he and Mr. Swarthout and the widow Ella—well, they seemed sort of thick for a time."

"Thick?"

"You know, friendly."

"I see. You mean going out to dinner and things like that."

"Exactly." He hesitated again. Glanced at the closed door as if somebody might have an ear pressed to the other side. "I'm told Grieves even went to the widow Ella's for dinner several times."

I rolled myself a cigarette. "What I'd like to know is if Mr. Grieves opened a checking or savings account here."

A tic appeared beneath his right eye. "That's what I was afraid of."

"I don't understand."

"Confidential information. If I gave that out without Mr. Swarthout's approval—"

"He'd put you on the slave ship?"

The tic stayed but at least the smile was wide and genuine. Then decorum got the best of him. "Confidential information is something we hold sacred here."

"That's good to know. I'd expect the same from my own bank."

"I'm sorry."

But he'd answered my question. He wouldn't have looked so put upon if he hadn't wanted to keep something secret from me. Something like a savings or checking account.

"You gave the impression that Swarthout and Ella and Grieves might have had some sort of falling out?"

"I did?"

"You said they were thick 'for a time.' "

"Oh, yes. I see. Well, that's correct. They spent a lot of time together—or so I'm told, you know how whispers spread in a workplace, people love gossip—but then apparently they stopped going around together."

"And you have no idea why?"

"Well, I'm not privy to that sort of information. Mr. Swarthout doesn't confide in me."

I stood up and shoved my hand over to him. He had an unexpectedly strong handshake. "I appreciate your time, Mr. Axminster."

"I hope I was helpful. I mean without divulging anything. I mean if you should ever have a conversation with Mr. Swarthout I hope you'll—"

"I'll tell him you refused to cooperate in any way."

"But that I was pleasant about it. Mr. Swarthout has a fit when his employees aren't polite."

"I'll bet Swarthout's unpleasant to his employees, though, isn't he?"

His face burned with all the anger he'd stored up for his boss. "Please don't put me on the spot."

"You weren't helpful in any way and you were one of the most polite gentlemen I've ever dealt with."

"I'd appreciate it if you'd say exactly that."

"That's exactly what I'll say. Thanks, Mr. Axminster."

❈

One place I've learned to stop by when I'm tracking somebody is the library. Not that the people I'm after are usually book readers but people on the run have need of different kinds of information and in most towns that means the libraries.

That's only one of the reasons I stop, of course. As much as I have great need of getting out of Washington after only a week or two there, I like to find out what's going on back in D.C. And libraries usually have the best collection of newspapers and magazines.

The size of the library in Junction City surprised me. It had the floor space and selection you'd expect in a much larger town. It was also busy for a weekday.

The librarian was a handsome woman of fifty-something, her gray hair done in a bun and her red dress possessing a touch of the regal. She had a smile like a beacon.

"Good morning, may I help you with something?"

"Yes, I'd appreciate that. You've got a real nice library here."

"Well, thank you. A wealthy farmer was thoughtful enough to remember us in his will. I taught him how to read and I guess he never forgot it."

I discreetly showed her my badge. I didn't want to attract any attention.

"My, federal. That's something we don't see much of around here."

"I'm actually looking for another federal man."

"You must mean Mr. Grieves." She had a wry, intelligent smile. "He took a liking to one of the young women who works here—a widow—and he sent her flowers every day for five days. That's something else we don't see much of around here. We'll be talking about that for years, I imagine." She was obviously amused by Grieves's grand gesture. "But Martha—who is very pretty, by the way—is no young naïf. She knows a professional ladies' man when she sees one."

"So she never went anywhere with him?"

"Wouldn't even let him walk her home. Her husband was something like that, a nice man but an eye for the ladies he couldn't control. Poor Martha suffered through their whole marriage because of that. So when Mr. Grieves tried courting her—he brought back too many unpleasant memories. So she shared the flowers with the churches around town. I doubt Mr. Grieves would've liked that if he'd known about it."

"Did he spend much time here, aside from trying to court Martha?"

"No, not really. He looked through magazines sometimes but that was about all. And he only did that because he was waiting for Martha to be free."

Grieves had become a legend in this town. But not all legends are good by any means.

"Was he always alone?"

She thought about this. "He always came in alone as I recall. But once I did see him talk for a few minutes to this little, nervous man who came in quite frequently. We never did get his name. Now, he was really a reader. The time Mr. Grieves talked to him, though, it didn't look like they saw eye to eye much. They had words of some kind. They kept their voices down but it was obvious that they were disagreeing about something."

"You said this little man came in frequently?"

"Yes. He'd always go right over to the newspaper section and take down the St. Louis paper. One day I asked him if he'd come from St. Louis and—Well, I can't say he actually cried but I'm sure I saw tears in his eyes. And then he started talking about how nice spring was here but that it was even nicer in St. Louis. He described what it was like to see the flowers bloom and how orchestras played in the parks and how handsome the big ships looked coming into the docks. He sounded so lonely. I wondered how a man like him—he was obviously a very different sort of man than Mr. Grieves—how the two of them had ever gotten connected."

While she wasn't giving me any startling information, I was starting to get a sense of "the little man" who played some sort of role in the swath Grieves had cut through town there.

I saw two women come in the front door. They walked directly to the front desk where I was talking to the librarian. I turned and looked at them. "I'll be done here right away, ladies."

They didn't look unduly happy about my presence.

"Can you remember the last time you saw Grieves?"

She hesitated. "Oh, at least two weeks ago."

"More flowers for Martha?"

"No, I think he'd learned his lesson by then." She snapped her fingers. "In fact, now that I think about it, he just stood right here at the front desk and looked around. You can see pretty much everything from here. He was obviously looking for somebody. I was thinking that it was that nice little man. But he wasn't here. And I'm just as glad. I just had the sense that he shouldn't be anywhere near Mr. Grieves. I just felt that Mr. Grieves was probably a bad influence on people."

I smiled. "You could be right about that."

I bid my adieus to the two ladies behind me—they looked very impatient—and then walked outside into the fresh air again.

One thing the little man was right about. It was hard to beat St. Louis in the springtime.

Chapter 13

Every once in a while you just walk into trouble. You don't expect it, you don't want it, you'd walk away from it double time if you had a chance, but there it is and through no fault of your own. Only later would I learn of the strange coincidence that had brought me to that place.

The name of the drinking emporium in the Lincoln Hotel was Time Out, the baseball reference being the motif of the place. The walls were lined with photographs of major league players of the day. There were at least six of Buck Ewing in his Troy Trojans baseball uniform (they needed an update; by then he played for the New York Giants); and Dude Esterbrook of the St. Louis Maroons; and Pud Galvin of the Buffalo Bisons who was, to me, the most overrated pitcher of the day. Bats, balls, even a catcher's mitt or two were displayed in small lighted areas. The rest of the place was appropriately dark.

The customers were mostly couples, twenties up to fifties. They all looked prosperous. Most of them were laughing, enjoying themselves. There was a player piano that played discreetly bouncy music to set a merry atmosphere. And the waiters in their white shirts, red vests, red arm garters, and fancy mustaches did their best to convince you that they were just as merry as the music.

According to all the books I'd read on alcoholism, saloons were a dangerous place for a nonimbiber to hang out in. Made sense. But sometimes I just liked to sit there and drink coffee and roll cigarettes and watch people. And try to fight off the worst memories of my drinking days. The unforgivable way I'd treated people sometimes, the humiliation and debasement of my own doing, and all the ridiculous fights I'd gotten into. I was one of those drunks who'd argue over anything and while I wasn't in danger of becoming a boxing champion, I had a violent urge to pound on somebody. Or maybe it was to be pounded on. Maybe punishment was what I was after, knowing what a shit I was.

The only couple not getting along was a pair to my right. A handsome couple, expensively dressed, she sober, he very drunk.

He was calling her some pretty filthy names. He was apparently under the impression that nobody else could hear him.

Except for kids coming to drag their dads or moms home, there's probably not much more sorrow in a saloon than when a man begins attacking his woman with words. Drink makes you crazy suspicious and crazy suspicious is pretty ugly to see or hear.

"Why don't you go table to table and screw every man in here, Nan?" the drunk said just as the waiter set down my coffee and beef sandwich.

The waiter, a stringy, bald fellow with big hands and raw knuckles, said, "You either keep him quiet, Mrs. Turner, or I'll have to get the bat and throw him out."

"Do you hear that, Glen? Are you happy now?" She

was all too well aware of how everybody in the small place was watching the drama.

He responded like a scolded schoolboy. He hung his head and started shaking it from side to side.

"Don't ever work in a saloon," the waiter said.

For the next ten minutes or so, there was peace. Two couples got up and danced to the player piano. The talk was low. And the drunk just sat there staring at his drink, silent.

Then he turned to his left and took a look at me.

"Who the hell you think you are, lookin' at my wife that way?"

"Oh, God, Glen, just turn around here. He wasn't looking at me."

"He wants to get you in bed is what he wants."

He was more pretty than handsome and more whiny than threatening. He wore a black suit of Edwardian cut with a forest-green vest of silk. On a riverboat he would have fit in with the cardsharps.

She was an appealing blonde, not quite beautiful, but stylish in a gray suit cut to tastefully display her slender but elegant body. City woman, most definitely.

"Now you turn around here, Glen, and forget all about him, you hear me?"

Everybody was watching again and watching eagerly. Not even the best stage entertainment was this good. This was real.

"Why don't we ask him to sit down with us?" Glen said, trying to sound crafty. He turned to me: "Come over here and sit down. My wife wants to meet you. It's her birthday. Maybe you'll be her present."

"Glen!"

But you know how drunks are. Nothing less than a two-by-four across the forehead was going to shut him up.

"That's right, everybody!" he said, mock-grandiose. "I am giving my wife the birthday present she wants most. Some dirty, uneducated, foul-smelling drifter!"

The waiter looked at me to see if I was going to respond. All I did was shrug. I'd been going to roll myself a cigarette but I figured now I'd be going.

"I'm very sorry about this," the woman said to me. "He gets very jealous."

"Oh, did you hear that?" the drunk said, again addressing the others at the tables. " 'He gets very jealous.' As if she never gives me any reason to get jealous. She always pretends she's this saint—but I think you know better, don't you?"

He erupted from his seat, turning to me before the waiter had time to scurry across the distance separating my table and the bar.

It happened this way: The drunk turns toward me, waving a fist. The wife virtually jumps on him, trying to stop him. I just sit there, waiting to see how to play it. The waiter cries for him to stop. The wife has such a tight grip on his coat sleeve that she tears it away. And that's when he unloads. He spits an enormous gob of hot spittle right across my nose. Instinct ejects me from my seat. Instinct also starts to propel me toward him. And to make a fist that is instantly ready to throw.

And that is when the waiter grabs my arm.

And that is when the drunk, after a spectacular circus-like wobble, falls a bit to his left, his head smacking the table so hard he breaks the legs of it. With nothing to break his fall, he goes right on down to the floor.

I don't take well to being spit upon. Probably a character flaw on my part. I wanted to smash his face in, do any damage his fall had left undone.

The waiter and a couple of male customers were dragging the drunk to his feet. I just wanted to be gone.

As I started toward the door, the drunk's wife hurried up to me and said, above all the noise of dredging up her husband, "I'm sorry this happened." And then she pressed a luscious breast against my arm. "And for what it's worth, I really would like to sleep with you."

Then she was gone, back to her drunken husband.

❂

Three blocks down the street, I saw them. There weren't that many of them, maybe four across and six deep, but they were men hardened and begrimed at the end of the day by the work they had just finished doing. They carried placards that read:

> DON'T DESERT US
> NO LOYALTY
> WE HAVE FAMILIES

The streets were lined with citizens who looked as if they weren't sure how to respond. Unions were still controversial. The tycoons had ordered their newspaper and magazine editors to make the whole idea of working people joining together something sinister and foreign. They usually meant Jews and Italians when they said foreign. Most of the time they went with the code word on the assumption that their readers would know what they meant.

The tycoons wanted people to think that working people weren't smart enough on their own to resent their low wages and dangerous conditions. They needed "outsiders" to tell them that.

So the citizens stood and watched, not waving their agreement but not expressing any disagreement, either.

Somebody said, "I'm all for them."

I looked down and there was Liz. She looked especially fetching in the dusk light. I particularly liked her blue hair ribbon. It was earnest and sweet and very very female.

"But I suppose you don't agree."

"No, I like to see people suffer."

"You look like the kind who would."

"In fact, I'd cut their wages in half and make them sleep outdoors in the winter."

"The territorial legislature agrees with just about everything you say. The robber barons bought them off a long time ago."

The picketers had begun to chant now: "Stay in town! Stay in town! Stay in town!"

"That's the sad thing. They don't get fair pay and the owner won't do anything about the working conditions—but they want to keep their jobs, anyway. They don't have any choice." I rolled myself a smoke as I talked.

The crowd's attitude had changed. Across the faces of the onlookers you then saw smiles and heard applause as the miners passed by us, headed for the end of the business district two blocks away.

The faces of the miners were less surly, too. Their work-grimed faces opened up with grins as they waved to friends and neighbors.

"It'll be a ghost town, just like everybody says," Liz said. Then: "Guess I'd better get back to work. I've got a little time tonight. I'll look up those issues for you that Grieves wanted."

I walked with her. "You ever been to the mansion where Grieves was staying?"

"You kidding? A working girl like me?"

"Exclusive territory, huh?"

"That's what they'd like people to think. But they've

got some pretty bad stuff going on out there. At least Grieves did. I hear he even brought in some very young girls."

We stood in front of the newspaper office.

"There's probably a good story in it. Folks were always curious about the place but Nickels, the man who owned it, never invited locals in. He figured owning a mine that was making a lot of money gave him the right to be a snob. He could barely put two English sentences together and even when he could afford Kentucky whiskey he preferred moonshine. But he didn't want to traffic with anybody who reminded him of when he'd been poor." She smiled. "I almost felt sorry for him. He'd give a few crumbs to the library and he'd always dress up in a tuxedo and top hat and give these long speeches about the arts. And people would snicker at him right in front of him. And when he'd finally leave, they'd laugh out loud and mock him. And then he went bust. He barely escaped with his life because by that time he owed everybody in town."

She nudged me in the ribs.

"Don't you be going out with any young girls."

She went inside the newspaper office. I watched her friendly little bottom all the way in until it vanished behind the door.

Chapter 14

I sat up reading magazines until I started going in and out of sleep right there in the rocking chair. Then I decided to make it official. I went to bed. And then of course couldn't get back to sleep right away.

I must have spent a long, useless hour trying to put together what I knew about Arnold Grieves's time there in town. He sure wasn't too concerned about his pregnant wife back home nor his assignment to find the counterfeiting ring working out in Junction City.

Finally, with no warning, sleep shut me down.

A furtive knock.

What the hell time was it?

Female voice: "Hurry. Hurry."

Some sort of trap?

I got up, grabbing my Colt as I eased out of bed, and walked to the door.

Female voice: "Please let me in."

I stood to the side of the door and opened it.

The only light was from a sconce in the hallway. She came in. She'd changed into a dark blue blouse and a long skirt. She had a fine body and groggy as I was my own body began to respond to hers.

I wondered where her husband was. Maybe he was waiting downstairs. Maybe she was just getting the door open so he could rush in and spit at me.

She couldn't see me as yet. I stepped behind her, gave her a nudge into the room and then closed the door.

"It's dark in here, Mr. Ford."

I went over and turned up the oil lamp.

"You aren't very talkative." The lamplight played gently on the nice cheekbones and the nice breasts.

I went over and sat on the edge of the bed. I used the Colt to point to the rocking chair. She carried a golden pint of some liquid. It had a champagne color. "You still haven't said a word," she said as she sat down.

"Why're you here?"

And she hiccupped. Just a little. Actually it was sort of cute. But that and the somewhat wobbly way she'd walked to the rocking chair spoke of a little too much alcohol.

"I came to apologize for my husband."

"He send you?"

She smiled. "You think anybody as jealous as he is would send me up to your room?" She shook her sweet head. "No, he's back in our hotel room, passed out as usual."

"So you just decided to come up here on your own?"

"Yes, though now that I'm here, I'm a little nervous." Then: "Say, would you be a gentleman and get us a couple of glasses?"

"I don't drink liquor if that's what you've got in mind."

"On the bureau. The bottle I brought. Pure apple juice from back East."

That actually sounded good. I was lucky to find two tin cups, no priceless glassware, of course.

I was pouring a cup for her when I heard the bed squeak. When I turned around she was lying on her side, an elbow propping her head up, looking just about irresistible.

"You're crazy, you know that? Or do you just want me to help you get rid of your husband? You tell him you came up here, he comes after me with a gun, and I'm forced to kill him. You're free again."

I handed her her apple juice. I'd sniffed it to be sure that was what it was and then I half emptied my own cup. She tilted hers back, too. "Don't you like it?"

"Tastes very good. Now you'd better get up and leave."

"A federal man. It must get awful lonely."

"C'mon, let's go."

She laughed. "You don't sound very convincing, Mr. Ford. I'm not real sure you actually want me to leave."

I couldn't disagree. I couldn't find much of a voice to argue with her.

She held a slender hand out and said, "At least come over and sit down next to me for a minute."

"Dammit, now. You're leaving."

I took two more steps and took hold of her hand. She was ready for me. She yanked me right down on top of her. Well, maybe I didn't put as much resistance in trying to stay upright as I could have. But then suddenly those kinds of thoughts went away.

I was lying next to her, hard against her, and she was pulling my head down to hers and we were kissing and—

I wanted to get even closer but—

"I know what you're thinking, Mr. Ford."

"How about calling me 'Noah.' "

"All right, Noah it is. What you're thinking is that I'm married—"

"—and drunk."

"Not drunk. Well, not big drunk. Just a little drunk."

"And maybe you'll wake up in the morning—"

"You don't think he cheats on me?" She laughed angrily. "He cheats on me every chance he gets. As long as he's sober enough to do it, he'll do it with anybody. And I mean anybody." The words were still slightly slurred but I saw what she meant about being only a "little" drunk. "You want to do it and I want to do it, Noah, so let's just do it."

She leaned back and studied my face.

"You look funny."

"It's just—"

It was one of the subjects that still hurt to talk about. In my drinking days I'd talked about it a lot. I'd emptied saloons talking about it.

"Just what, Noah?"

I sighed. "Adultery."

"Adultery? God, don't use that word. I hate the word. We're just having some fun. Adultery—all I can think of is burning in hell."

"My wife—she used to cheat on me all the time. I was gone a lot. I came home one day and found her. And I realized then that when you're married you shouldn't cheat. Walk away from the marriage if you have to— but don't cheat."

She laughed. "Just my luck. I'm in bed with a minister." Then, putting her hand behind my head and pulling it toward her: "He spit in your face, Noah. And don't think he did it just because he was drunk. He'd do the same thing sober." Then, her free hand slipping down to my crotch: "Now that's a nice big one, Noah. Let's not waste it."

But I wasn't listening anymore. All sensation was now in my crotch. I was one singular piece of need. She was more skilled than passionate but who was I to complain? The only company I'd kept for most of the last month was my horse. So I was grateful even though I knew I was just part of some stupid game she and her husband had apparently been playing for some years now.

And then it did the deed, the juice she'd given me. None of that stuff that just throws you to the floor. More subtle, as was to be expected from a well-bred woman. I'd have to get the name of the drug she'd used on me. Might come in handy some day.

❖

I wasn't sure of the time when I finally woke up. All I knew was that somebody seemed to be tossing trees against my door. That thunderous. There was just enough dawning light to see that Nan had ripped through all my clothing, bureau drawers, saddlebags. And even the clothes I'd been wearing, all the pockets turned out.

I wondered who the hell she really was.

But the pounding on my door continued and then I was up and struggling into my trousers and there was Knut. Gasping a bit. He must have been running.

"You better get over to the jail fast, Noah."

"What is it?"

"Somebody murdered Molly Kincaid."

"Wasn't she in her cell?"

"Yeah, that's the strange thing. They killed her right in her cell."

PART TWO

Chapter 15

Even though the usual wake-up time for the town was still about an hour away, the frosty morning was already filled with people, at least in the business area where the hotels were.

There was a crowd outside the sheriff's office. A lot of people were drinking steaming coffee out of tin cups. A deputy I didn't recognize was ordering them to stand farther back from the door because the funeral wagon would be arriving soon.

I didn't blame them. Regular death is pretty exciting. Death by murder is fifty times better. Especially if the death was visited upon the female of the species and especially if she was young and pretty. You live in any city with a tabloid and you know that that's what keeps them in business. You half suspect they go out and commit the grisly murders themselves just to stay in business.

I didn't know who the deputy was but he seemed to recognize me. He waved me inside.

The small office was crowded. Longsworth, the young attorney, was there with his treasure chest of a briefcase. A minister clutching a Bible to his chest would have looked reverent if he hadn't been smoking a cigar. And a nurse in white was saying to nobody in particular, "There just wasn't anything we could do to help her. They didn't find her until it was too late."

But it was the two standing in the corner, next to the American flag, who interested me most. The widow Ella Coltrane and the wealthiest man in town, Nels Swarthout. He saw me first and glared in my direction. She followed his glare with her own. Grieves might have had a relationship with her but it was doubtful I would.

I wondered how they'd gotten the news so quickly, given that their fine big homes were on the outskirts of town. Even more I wondered why they would be there at all. What interest did they have in Molly Kincaid? They didn't look like the kind of tabloid readers who showed up at every murder.

Terhurne burst from the people packing the inner doorway to the jail cell. When he saw me, his face took on a radiance that was almost religious. Few people had ever looked so happy to see me. Hell, my parents had never looked that happy to see me.

"Let's us go get some coffee and have a smoke, Noah."

I believe that was the first time he'd ever spoken my first name.

I wondered what the hell he wanted from me.

He gave me a little shove, which irritated the hell out of me. I turned around and gave him the same kind of glare that Ella and Swarthout had put on me.

"Sorry, I'm just in kind of a hurry."

Hurry to get out of here, I thought. I remembered his discomfort around blood. How'd poor Molly been killed?

"If I don't figure this thing out damned fast, there goes my reelection."

Politicians are pretty much the same, whether they be sheriffs, governors, or presidents. They do best the things that are in their own self-interest. While he was worried about his career, I was thinking about the sad, oddly fragile girl named Molly.

"There's one man in town here who's jumping up and down this morning, I'll tell you that. His name's Rafferty." He spoke around a lumpy mouthful of pancake and over-easy egg. He jabbed his fork at me from time to time for emphasis. "A little gal is supposedly sleeping in one of my cells and somebody gets in and kills her. I can hear that bastard up there on the stump now. 'Right in his own cell while he was home sleeping off a—well, I won't say it but we all know how the sheriff likes to support the liquor industry, don't we?' That was a joke from the last election."

We sat in the Imperial, the same place where I first saw Swarthout and Ella, where the elite, as they say, meet to eat. It was now getting on to seven a.m. so the restaurant was starting to fill up quickly. From what I could hear of the talk around me, the only subject was Molly Kincaid being murdered in her cell.

"I hate to interrupt you, Terhurne, but maybe you could fill me in on what happened."

He leaned forward and said, "I know you think I'm a callous bastard, Ford. But look at it this way. This town deserves the best lawman it can get."

"And that could only be you."

"You're one sarcastic bastard, you know that?"

"Look, just tell me what happened."

He knew they were looking at him. A lot of men whose attire and bearing told you that they were important in that little town were nodding in his direction.

He was going to become, at best, a joke. And at worst a true villain.

He said, in a gravelly low voice, "I don't know what happened. That's the thing. Hayden went over to the café where we get meals for the prisoners. And there's this new waitress there with these milk jugs you just wouldn't believe and—"

I tried not to groan. "So it's five o'clock in the morning and Hayden figures he'll not only get breakfast, he'll put in a little time sniffing around the new girl. And he leaves the office unlocked because it's too much trouble to unlock it when he comes back with an armload of breakfast."

"You sound like you were there."

"So the killer sneaks in, grabs the key, and lets himself into her cell."

"And kills her."

I had to say it. "You might as well turn in that badge right now."

He got twenty years older right in front of me. "That bad?"

"At least that bad. You can't even protect a young woman in your own jail?"

He punched a fist into an open palm. "I never should've hired Hayden. My damned sister bred six morons. It's in descending order. By the time you get to the sixth, which is Hayden, they can't take a piss without three people helpin' 'em."

He was just finishing up this round of understandable self-pity when a lanky man in a blue suit and a grim New England face walked in and came straight to the table.

"Oh, just what I need."

"Who is he?" I said as I watched the bald man advance on us.

"The mayor."

"Good morning, gentlemen. Ford, we haven't met."
He shoved a hand at me and we shook. "I'm Bryant
Willis, mayor of this fine town."

I smiled. "You've got my vote."

"This is hardly a time for levity."

"No, it isn't. But if you've come over to pound on our
friend Terhurne here, he's doing a damned good job of it
himself and he doesn't need any reinforcement."

"As a federal man, I'd think you'd be disgusted by
this kind of shoddy work."

I shrugged. "The thing is, Mayor, there isn't a lawman, a senator, or even a president who hasn't done
something stupid in his career. And I suspect the same
thing could be said for mayors. So he made a mistake
and something terrible happened. Like I said, he's well
aware of that."

"I'm shocked you would defend his stupidity. He
hired Hayden over our objections. But Terhurne here
has a bully side to him and he managed to browbeat the
town council long enough to get his way."

"I'll tell you what, Mayor, if it'll make you feel any
better, I'll throw in with Terhurne here and help him out
with the investigation. You can wire D.C. and ask about
my record as an investigator."

"Why would you do that?"

"Simple. Vested interest. I think Molly was killed by
the same person or persons I'm after."

"I can tell the council this?"

"Be my guest."

"They'll want me to fire Terhurne here."

I could see Terhurne forcing himself to sit quietly as
we discussed him. He had enough rage inside to kill
four or five men with his fists and right on the spot. At
that moment all the rage was surging in him but all he

could do was sit still like a good citizen and hear himself run down by the mayor.

Willis scowled at Terhurne. "I sure hope you won't be stupid enough to run for election again, Terhurne. Because right now my arthritic old mother could beat you three to one."

"You've been waiting for this a long time, Willis. And you finally got your wish." The self-pity in Terhurne's voice just made it worse.

"The point is, Mayor," I said, "as soon as we leave here, Terhurne and I start on our investigation. And I hope to have a written report on your desk within twenty-four hours to let you and the council know how things are going."

"You hear that, Terhurne? That's a real lawman talking. A professional lawman. Something you'll never be."

He offered his hand again and we shook. "The folks in D.C. should be damned proud of you." This was the voice he used when he was handing out the award for Not Farting in Church Oftener Than Once a Month given by the local Kiwanis club.

Even with the mayor gone, Terhurne was still sullen. "You both made me sound like I'm an imbecile. I didn't ask you to step in. I don't need no favors."

"No, but I do. I need you to help me find out what happened to Grieves."

"I still don't think that has anything to do with Molly."

"No? Then why did she mention his name when she was holding a razor to my throat?"

"It doesn't mean that it had anything to do with murdering her."

I leaned over and said, "You want me to start telling everybody that I think you should be fired before the election?"

"You just told the mayor—"

"I can always tell him you were holding a gun on me under the table."

He started to call me a name but apparently couldn't come up with one vile enough. He sank in his chair.

"I'm running this investigation, Terhurne. And if you don't help me, I'll give a statement to the paper about what an incompetent you are."

He started to call me another name but I spoke first. "How many brothels you have in town?"

"Three. Why? What's that got to do with anything?"

"Which is the best one?"

"Brandy Bowen's. But—"

"I need directions."

"What's Brandy got to do—"

"Because Grieves probably went there a few times. Only the finest for our boy Grieves. I want to see if she can help me with anything."

He smirked. "So this is how you 'professional boys' do it, huh? A whorehouse is the best you can come up with?"

I stood up. "And I'm going to be needing a lot more information. So keep yourself easy to find."

I threw some money on the table and left.

❖

I wanted to see for myself where Molly had been murdered. A deputy nodded courteously when I came in. He said, "Afraid the sheriff isn't here right now. My name's Cliff Needham but I'm just a deputy."

Needham was a middle-aged man in a boiled white shirt, a string tie, a full head of dark-brown hair and a mild face. The eyes were blue and intelligent. If he had been on duty, Molly would still be alive.

I showed him my badge and he came out from around the desk and shook my hand. "Hearing some good things about you, Mr. Ford."

"Noah'll do fine."

"Any way I can help you, Noah, I'll be glad to."

"I'd like to look around the cell where Miss Kincaid was."

He smiled. "You're making it easy for me."

He walked back to the desk, opened a drawer, pulled out a ring of keys, and then reached out and handed them to me.

"You like a cup of coffee?"

"Appreciate it, Cliff. But I can get my own."

I walked over and got myself a cup and started filling it. "You hear anything new about her being killed?"

"Some people think Hayden might have done it. But I'm pretty sure he didn't."

"Why not?"

He hesitated, uncomfortable. "Well, Hayden isn't real mature about things. He's a nice kid but he isn't an adult yet, if you understand what I mean."

"Yeah, that's the impression I had, too."

"If Hayden killed her, he would've confessed by now."

"You sure about that?"

"Well, if he didn't confess you'd at least be able to tell it on him. He'd be all jittery and edgy. And he'd confess real soon."

"You sound pretty sure."

"He grew up next door to me. I've known him since he was about two. He can't keep a secret and if he does anything bad, he comes right to you and tells you. Besides, he's got that young gal at the café as his alibi."

"Maybe she's lying."

He laughed. "You got it wrong. He's sweet on her

but she ain't sweet on him. She already got one of the Hayworth boys to go around with. Believe me, Hayden doesn't have a chance against a Hayworth boy."

❇

Five minutes later I was in the cell where Molly had been murdered. There was a splash of blood on the wall and some strands of her hair in the blood. The killer had pounded her head against the wall, which wouldn't have been hard to do, given Molly's size. According to the doc's report, which Cliff had shown me a few minutes earlier; Molly had died of a brain injury. There had also been faint bruising on her neck, as if the killer had started to strangle her but stopped.

Farther down you could see more blood. Molly must have slid down the wall after losing consciousness.

I sorted through the bed clothes, I scanned the walls for any kind of abrasion or scratch, I got down on my hands and knees and searched under the cots. I probably wouldn't have noticed it if it hadn't made a scraping sound against the floor. Just a tiny scrape.

I pulled my hand out from beneath the cot and looked at a button. That was my first impression of it, anyway, a miniscule dot of silver. It looked ornamental, not practical. But I had no idea what it was.

❇

"Sorry, Noah, I sure don't know what it is. There're a lot of people in and out of those cells. Preachers and women from Salvation Army and then of course the prisoners themselves. You're seein' us at low tide. Usually every one of them cells is filled." He pushed his face closer to where the silver lay in my palm. "Could be off a fancy boot of some kind. One of them real fussy ones they make up for ya in Denver. I seen 'em decorated like this a lot of times."

"How about an envelope to put this in?"

"Sure thing."

When I had the unidentified silver dot in the envelope, and the envelope in my back pocket, I thanked Cliff and left.

I ran into Knut walking toward the office. "Sorry I wasn't around when they found Molly. Home sound asleep."

"Wouldn't worry about it, Knut. You can't be on duty twenty-four hours a day."

He frowned. "Between you and me, somebody should be."

Terhurne was damned lucky to have an assistant deputy who cared about his job the way Terhurne should have.

The railroad depot was noisy, crowded, and smelly. One thing nobody's figured out—unless you're traveling in a private rail car—is how to keep very clean on long train rides. So on a substantial trip, body odors of various kinds begin to accumulate. The railroads advertise that things are a lot better than they used to be but then we know about advertising, don't we?

The cigars being smoked didn't help the depot atmosphere much, either. It seemed everybody over the age of two was puffing away.

Several elderly Comanches, an enormous family of Irishers, three middle-aged men in the loud suits and dusty derbies of drummers, and various weary-looking single travelers of just about every age filled the benches where passengers waited to depart. And then there were the kids. With their fresh faces, their noisy games, and their laughter, they looked as if they belonged to a species separate from the one the adults belonged to. A new species, these kids were, one that neither travel nor boredom could wear down. Their energy was almost threatening.

"You work days, sir?" I said to the buzzard-like face behind the ticket cage. The man was scrawny inside his gray uniform shirt and beneath his blue cap with the railroad logo riding bold above the bill.

"And you'd be who?" Then he stopped himself. "You'd be that federal man."

"And you'd be the man who works days?"

"I would be. If it's any of your business."

"You always this friendly?"

"I don't like federales."

"Well, I guess we're even up. I don't like cranky old bastards."

He spat some chaw down into an unseen spittoon. Either that or he had a hell of a messy floor.

"The name is Duncan Winters in case you want to write it down in that little book of yours. And don't call me Dunc. I hate Dunc. Teacher give me that name way back when I lived in New Hampshire when I was seven. I figured I'd have a new start out here, telling everybody to call me Duncan. But my little brothers and sisters kept calling me Dunc, so it started up here all over again." He thought a moment: "And you want me to tell you what?"

I smiled. "Maybe you're not as much of an asshole as I thought. Maybe you're going to cooperate and I won't have to take you outside and slam your head against the tracks."

He smiled right back. "You do and I'll sue you federales for every penny you got."

"A federal man sleep with your wife one time, did he?"

"Damned near. He shot my brother in the back and got away with it."

Not much anybody could say to that. "I'm going to take your word for that, Duncan. And I'm going to apologize for it."

"And don't give me that one bad apple bullshit, either. Federales are as bad as Texas Rangers. Outlaws, all of them. I had a Mex wife and them Rangers never let me be."

You heard this just about everywhere in the West, people with grudges, a lot of them deserved, against various law enforcement men.

"Duncan, I'm here to ask you questions about another federal man named Grieves."

"Grieves. Now there was an asshole if there ever was one."

"He give you trouble?"

"No trouble. Just walked around like he owned the place."

"You see him more than once?"

"Just a couple times. But that was plenty for me."

"I was going to ask you if you remember the day he came."

"The way he treated the colored help? We all get along here. He was snappin' his fingers and orderin' everybody around. Even called Harry over there a dirty name a couple times."

Good old Grieves. I was getting a picture of a man who made it even easier to hate federal men.

"You say you saw him a couple of times. Why'd he come back?"

Another well-fired volley of chaw. "Wanted to know about the Pine Lake Resort."

"What's that?"

"Place rich people used to stay. Cost more to stay there a week than I make in three months. We even got a few famous people goin' there until all the trouble started."

"What happened?"

"They had murders and then they had cholera. Two days and somethin' like forty people died. And then they had a fire that burned down about a fourth of it. Lit like a message from the Lord. Shut the place down and it's never opened again."

"He didn't seem to know that?"

"Oh, he knew it was shut down. He wanted to know if there was any kind of train that went even close to there. Hell, no, there isn't."

"Wonder why he wanted to know that?" I was talking to myself.

"You 'bout done gabbin', mister?"

The voice came from behind me. A formidable older man who would probably be formidable on his deathbed. That big, that much mean in his eyes.

"You didn't see him again?"

"No," Duncan not Dunc said, "and I never want to again, either."

❖

Noah Ford had been in Junction City a while before Grieves heard about it. So the federales had finally come looking for Grieves. This gave great secret pleasure to Dobbs.

Apparently this Noah Ford was a man Grieves feared. On the night he got the news, Grieves told Dobbs about several of Ford's successes as a human tracker. Grieves seemed to have no doubt that Ford would find him. And very soon now.

Grieves spent the rest of the night in the vast, empty resort talking to the gunny he considered the best he'd hired. A man named Parsons. Parsons was eager for the job. His eagerness sickened Dobbs. Parsons exhibited the same kind of childish excitement Grieves had when he'd killed the horse.

By this time, Dobbs felt that he was surrounded by several evil and insane children. But he had to be careful. Just about everything he did and said in those days seemed to irritate, even infuriate Grieves.

He had to be very, very careful or Grieves would turn on him.

Chapter 16

Brothels come in all sizes, shapes, and colors, just like the girls and women inside. There was a madam who had a whole chain of whorehouses in soddies out in North Dakota Territory. She served mostly buffalo hunters and railroad workers. One of the agency's best informants was a seventy-year-old woman who operated from under an alley stairwell and took care of men who preferred the company of, apparently, the elderly.

Brandy Bowen, madam, resembled a witch. The sharp features, the wild dark hair, the imperious blue eyes. She wore a severely cut black dress that only emphasized her skinny, angular shape. She opened the front door then stood in it, as if blocking it.

"The girls don't come down for another hour."

"It's actually you I wanted to see."

She looked startled. "You want to go upstairs with me? I've got to be honest with you, mister. I'm workin' on a bad case of the clap."

Now it was my turn to be startled. The seventy-year-old started sounding a lot better than the woman in front of me.

I showed the badge.

"We pay Terhurne. He said that included federales."

"I'm not here for a payoff. I'm here to ask you about a federal agent named Arnold Grieves."

She whinnied. That's the only way I can describe the sound. A whinny. "I sure hope you spend money like he does. He's a party man. Boom boom boom."

" 'Boom boom boom.' I guess I don't know what that means."

"I was just drinking some coffee. You want some?"

"I'd appreciate it."

Some brothels are simply shacks or weathered old houses without the mercy of decoration. Some, like those in San Francisco, are fussily decorated to resemble Parisian parlors for the wealthy. Brandy's resembled a standard American home, right down to the bad paintings you could order three for two dollars from the Sears catalog if your town didn't yet have a store. A couple of windows were open. The air smelled clean. She took me out to the kitchen. A rather hefty woman in a nightgown that displayed pretty much everything was pouring herself a cup of coffee. "You opening early this morning, Brandy?" she asked.

"Copper," Brandy said.

"Trouble?"

"Nope. Scoot."

These two had reduced verbal communication to a minimum.

The woman scooted.

"Name's Dot if you're interested."

"I'll pass."

"You like girls?"   ·

"Most of the time. Right now I need to talk about Grieves."

She served us coffee. We sat at a small table. The room was sunny, clean, well organized, new cabinets, counters, well pump, and large ice box. The double stove bore the Sears name.

"Nice place here." I was falling into her own minimal way of talking.

"Spic and span. Clean as a whistle. Like brand new. That's why I resent having the clap. I always give the girls hell if they miss their monthly checkup with the doc in town and then I'm the one that goes and gets somethin'. Pisses me off. Doc says he can clear it up fast and all but it still sets a bad example for the girls."

The coffee was good.

"One more thing about Dot. She spent some time down in Mexico. She learned some pretty unique tricks down there."

"You're a pretty good salesman."

"I've got the best girls in three hundred miles, is what I always say. I've got a fatty goes nearly three hundred pounds and I've got a skinny that looks like she's about fourteen. And the skinny one's got a beautiful face on her, too. Angel face. Her problem is tits. She's about the flattest little thing I ever saw."

"How about Grieves? He pretty flat?"

She whinnied again. "I like a man with a sense of humor." She sat back. In the sunshine through the windows her hair looked like a fright wig. Only now did I realize that it was badly dyed. She was probably gray.

"He was pretty loud. At least when he was here. Liked to make believe he was at this big party. Some of the customers liked it, others kind of resented he took over everything down here. That's the part that pissed me off. A shy little man comes in, he's nervous about being here in the first place, he don't want somebody like Grieves makin' him drink toasts and sing songs and everything. We got a piano in the parlor and Bobby the colored bouncer, he plays a fine piano. Grieves was always givin' him money to play one song or the other. And he was forever yellin' that 'boom boom boom' thing."

"What was that all about?"

"Couldn't tell you. One night he brought this real quiet guy along. Guy seemed embarrassed about bein' here. We get our fair share of them. He kept tryin' to get the shy one to join in all the singing and such but he wouldn't—until Grieves gave him some wine and then the shy one got as loud and obnoxious as Grieves. Grieves also kept huggin' everybody and sayin' 'boom boom boom' and then he'd say nobody was better at 'boom boom boom' than his friend here."

"When's the last time Grieves was here?"

"I'd have to think about it."

She sat and sipped her coffee. "Two and a half weeks ago."

"Where'd you get that figure?"

"Marie. Her birthday. The big one I mentioned. She's got her own little stable of regulars and they all showed up to help her celebrate. Grieves was here with his friend again. The 'boom boom boom' one. He was pretty drunk and ugly. He made some remark about Marie's weight and this big guy who likes Marie—he claims to have been a bear wrestler in the Yukon—he grabbed Grieves and told him to apologize to Marie. Grieves showed the man his badge but it didn't matter. Man wasn't impressed. He made Grieves apologize. Then the two of them got real shit-faced and became best buddies in the world. You know how drunks are."

"How about describing the quiet guy?"

She picked something from between her teeth with a craggy fingernail. She examined it. I thought maybe we'd have a discussion about it, the time she spent on it. Then she lowered her hand beneath the table top, made a wiping motion and brought the hand back up again. "Sandy haired, little, dark, but his name wasn't Eye-talian or nothing. And one of his eyes is glass. Blue. Except it doesn't fit exactly right. He plays with it a lot around the edges of his eye."

Not an easy fellow to miss.

Dot came back. "Excuse me but Hattie's sick to her stomach again. You want me to take her to the doctor?"

"Better not be that damned influenza. That costs me more money than clap." Then: "I better get upstairs, Mr. Ford."

I told her where I was staying.

"You should take advantage of my gals while you can. Soon as the mine shuts down for good, we'll be long gone."

She never stopped plugging.

❁

I was about half a block away from the good madam's when I heard the slap-slap of small feet. Being the distrustful sort, my hand dropped to my Colt—people with bad intent can have small feet, too—and I turned to see who was coming so fast at my back.

The rest of her was as small as her feet, a freckled prairie girl in a blue gingham dress and pigtails. "I heard you talking back there, mister."

When she caught up with me, she grabbed my arm and leaned against me, all out of breath.

She looked up at me smiling as she tried to get her wind again. "I never was much of a runner. My brothers back on the farm always made fun of me."

"Feeling better now?" I asked after a minute or so.

"Sorry," she said, taking one last gasp of ragged

breath. Then she seemed to be all right. "I wanted to tell you about Grieves's friend."

"Grieves's friend?"

"Uh-huh. See, when Brandy said he was sort of a bad drunk, he was. But he stayed with me and kind of sobered up. And then he was real nice. I heard you askin' questions about him so I figured I might as well add my part, too."

She slid her arm through mine. "You mind being seen on the street with a lady of ill repute?"

I laughed. "Not unless you mind being seen on the street with a *man* of ill repute."

"Then I guess we're even up, huh?" She gave my arm a little squeeze as we walked amidst the shade trees and the noisy knots of wee ones playing all sorts of wee-one games. You could smell wash on clotheslines, that heady clean scent, and pies on window sills cooling off for supper. A smart-looking carriage went by driven by a little old lady who wielded a pretty savage whip.

"He was sweet. After he started sobering up, I mean."

"He talk much?"

"A lot. He told me about New Hampshire where he grew up and how his first wife died and how he was coming up on fifty and had never gotten to do much with his life. And then he started crying."

"That's strange. Don't you think?"

"Not so much, really. A lot of men cry when they see us girls. They tell us things they'd never tell anybody else."

"Mind if I ask what he was crying about?"

"Look at that butterfly. I've never seen one like that before." Then: "Got sidetracked, sorry. Well, what he was crying about, he never really got specific, you understand, he just said he'd done something he shouldn't have and that he wished he could get out of it but that Grieves wouldn't let him."

"He didn't seem to like Grieves?"

"He was afraid of him and didn't trust him. And that's just how he put it. He said that Grieves was a very dangerous man."

"But he didn't tell you what he'd done that he wished he hadn't?"

"Just that he was thinking of going back home."

"Did he leave with Grieves?"

"Yes. I was wondering—after all he'd said about Grieves—how he'd act around him when they met up downstairs again. It was sort of sad. When they had their last drink in the parlor it was right after dawn and Grieves was in this real bad mood and made a lot of cruel jokes about him. I thought maybe he'd stand up for himself. But he didn't. He just sort of took it and didn't say much but you could tell everybody down there was embarrassed for him. But nobody said anything. Grieves was real scary, real hungover and angry. Then they just left."

We'd come to the end of the long block.

"Well, I just wanted to tell you that. Thought you should know."

"I appreciate it."

She slid her arm from mine. In the sunlight her freckles made her look thirteen or fourteen, though around the eyes now I could see the faint wrinkles that started with age twenty or so.

"You wouldn't want to come back and help me do my laundry, would you?"

"You do your own?"

"Are you fooling? Every girl does her own. Her clothes and her sheets. Brandy runs the place like a boot camp, though she's actually a nice woman."

"Thanks for talking to me."

She nodded and turned back toward the brothel. I watched her for a time, a sunflower of a girl. For a few yards there she even gave up walking and took up skipping.

❖

I stopped at the livery and asked the man there to draw me a map to Swarthout's mansion that Grieves had stayed in. He said he'd have it ready by the time I got back.

My next stop was the newspaper where Liz Thayer was at the counter sorting a large stack of flyers into numbers of what appeared to be twenty-five. She was alone in the ink-smelling shop. The press sat like a mute animal. She didn't look up to see who I was. She just shook her head not to be disturbed. She would have given the president and the pope the same dismissive shake of the head.

When she was done, she looked up and said, "Oh. You."

"More or less."

"You're wondering if I had time to find those two back issues that Grieves was interested in."

"That's one reason to be here. Another is to say hello."

Her eyes smiled. "You never give up, huh?"

"I'm not that old. And I can bring affidavits signed by mostly respectable women if you'd like to see them."

"The key word there is 'mostly' I suspect."

"None of us is without sin."

She laughed. "You're full of beans, you know that?"

"Just a lonely pilgrim trying to find shelter from the storm."

This time she giggled. "You are hopeless, Ford. You know that? Anyway, you could do a lot better than me."

She'd just started to say more when the front door opened up, the bell above it ringing, and a middle-aged woman in a bonnet and matching gingham dress came in.

"Just a minute, Noah. I'll be right with you, Mrs. Carstairs."

She hurried over to a desk piled high with books, papers, and pamphlets. The pile looked about to capsize and slide to the floor. She didn't even try to search through it. She went instead to the chair that was pushed into the desk. The pile there was much more modest. There was actual hope of finding what you were looking for. She only had to go through it twice.

Meanwhile, Mrs. Carstairs and I had one of those strained conversations that people feel compelled to have.

"Nice day."

"Sure is," I said.

"Last year this time we had a blizzard."

"Blizzards. I've had enough of them for a lifetime."

"My husband got lost in one once."

"Did they ever find him?"

She looked affronted. "Gosh sakes, yes. You don't think we'd just leave him out there, do you?"

Liz rescued me. "Here are the two papers he was interested in."

"I owe you anything?"

"I'm in sort of a hurry," Mrs. Carstairs said.

"Her husband was lost in a blizzard once."

"Yes, I know, Noah. I was ten at the time and I was one of the searchers."

"That's why we always bring our printing business here. Because her whole family searched for him. A lot of others turned back because it was so cold and bitter. But not the Thayers."

❁

Longsworth caught up with me as I left the newspaper office and turned into an alley that was a shortcut. As always he carried the briefcase that appeared to be loaded down with bricks. He also carried his eternal frown.

"I suppose you know what's going on."

He made it sound like an accusation.

"Nothing's going on, to answer my own question. Nobody's trying to find out who murdered that girl and her uncle."

"Well, I'm trying to find out."

"You are?" He seemed genuinely surprised. "Terhurne didn't tell me that."

"Where'd you see Terhurne?"

"That's my point, Mr. Ford." He wasn't much good at sarcasm. Sarcasm you have to ease back a little to make it effective. He used it like a board across the mouth. "I saw him in a saloon where he was playing cards. I think you'll have to have a talk with him."

He was the snitch we all hated in grade school. He'd wait until the classroom had emptied and then go up to the teacher and tell her all sorts of things about the immature brats he had to spend his days with. She wouldn't even ask him for this information. But he'd give it to her, anyway.

"Maybe he was just taking a break."

"Some break. He's been taking it ever since I got to town here. The fact is, he's lazy. People accuse him of all kinds of things but they never seem to see his biggest fault—he's a loafer."

I was tired of him and tired of that conversation. But then he made it all worthwhile: "You ever hear of a farmer named Tucker?"

I shook my head.

"Well, he stopped by my office on a completely different matter this morning and in the course of conversation, he talked about seeing Molly and her uncle and Grieves out by a rock quarry. And he said they were blowing the hell out of the place. He was pretty sure they were using dynamite."

He'd finally said something that interested me. "Where's this rock quarry?"

He told me.

"And when did this Tucker see them?"

He gave me a date.

"He see anybody else with them?"

"No. But isn't that enough? Maybe Grieves had a reason to kill her. And maybe that's what he did. Just snuck back into town here and killed her uncle and her."

"Just because they were all together blowing up parts of a rock quarry?"

Buggies and wagons creaked and rattled along the streets in the midday rush.

"Well, they were killed for some reason, Mr. Ford. And right now the only person we can tie them to is Grieves. That's worth looking into, I'd say."

"And I agree with you."

"You do?" He sounded shocked. He was apparently not used to winning arguments.

And what he'd told me was in fact interesting. Grieves and Molly and Uncle Bob. Working some kind of deal, no doubt. Right then, it was nothing more than a theory but the only theory we had.

"I hope you'll take care of this personally."

"I will. I promise. I appreciate the information."

He sighed. "I'm sorry if I'm a little rough on Terhurne. But he is a lazy bastard." Then: "She sure was a beauty."

"She had one of those faces."

"Yeah. Launch a thousand daydreams. Good material for the bedroom and the kitchen, too. You ever hear her talk? She had a voice like an angel."

I laughed gently. I was now embarrassed that we were having this conversation. Starting to make me nervous. "I think you'd better go find yourself a woman, Longsworth. A live one."

I nodded goodbye and turned to walk away when the two rifle shots cracked through the day from a roof across the street. The only thing that saved me was the uneven board on the sidewalk. The toe of my boot shoved against it just as the bullets were fired. I didn't trip but I did stumble forward. The shots were close enough to sing as they slashed by me.

The shooter had to have seen that he missed me. I dropped the material I'd been carrying and started to rush across the street only to find that a horse pulling a buggy had gone loco because of the shots and was now bucking up and down in the air. The old woman inside was screaming for help.

Then she did a foolish thing. As the horse continued to buck, the old woman tried to get down from the buggy. At the least, she could break a bone or two. She might even get a concussion if she fell headfirst and smacked her head on the ground.

No one else was in sight. I didn't have any choice but to stop, jump up, and grab the lines in order to pull the animal down and settle him as fast as I could. And it wasn't a simple job.

By the time I'd calmed both the old woman and the horse down, the shooter was long gone.

But I had no doubt who'd sent him. Grieves had decided to get rid of me.

Then Longsworth was there. Everything had happened so fast I'd forgotten about him.

He looked pale, shaken. "You know some real bad people, Ford."

I smiled. "Yeah, I guess I do at that."

❄

I found a park bench about a block away. It sat beneath the awning of a barbershop. Every time the door opened a man came out smelling like bay rum. The aroma always reminded me of living in Baltimore after the war with my wife. The memories were good then. Or maybe the illusions. Maybe my good memories were nothing more than things I hadn't cared to acknowledge to myself. Maybe those are the best memories of all.

The papers Liz had found were interesting. I found a story dealing with the glory days of the Pine Lake Resort. All the important people who'd stayed there. Some of the romances. The hunting and fishing trophies given out. And then the murders, the cholera attack, the fire that finally shut them down. Very grim. The hook of the story was that the town was searching hard for somebody to open the resort up again but had so far not found any takers.

I found a second story that was even more interesting. It discussed a former Army scientist, Mr. Nathan Dobbs, who had retired for health reasons and who had decided to settle in the West. The story said that there was some suspicion that the scientist had actually been prompted to retire by the church he had recently joined.

The church believed in pacifism and apparently Dobbs had become a devout believer.

An hour later I stood on a bluff staring down into the pit of a rock quarry that was backed by a limestone cliff that was as tall as the surrounding aspens.

I knew just enough about munitions, and specifically all the attempts that had been made with grenade-like weapons, to be curious about what I'd find that day.

Ever since the fifteenth century, military munitions men had been trying to create a handheld bomb that you could use in close combat. The problem was that every single time the grenade-like weapon was re-created it had the same problem. A good deal of the time the weapon exploded before the soldier could throw it. Napoleon, ever the optimist, thought he could solve this by enlisting soldiers who were tall and strong and could hurl the grenades great distances over the heads of their fellow soldiers, thus keeping everybody safe. He didn't have any better luck than his predecessors. No matter how tall and strong these soldiers were, they couldn't throw the grenades fast enough to avoid killing themselves.

It was well known that several countries, including the United States, were developing multiple variations on the basic grenade. Germany was building another enormous army, which made all of Europe uneasy. All kinds of weapons were under development at that time including, in Germany, a cannon that was said to be a weapon that could cause unheard-of destruction. So men like Dobbs were working hard to prepare for any emergency.

The man next to me in the bib overalls and wide

straw hat was a Mr. Averill Tucker. The corncob pipe he smoked looked to be at least as old as he was, which I estimated to be sixty-something.

From as high up as we were the scarred quarry looked very much like the New England quarry where the dinosaur bones had been discovered a few years back. They'd reconstructed a nearly perfect dinosaur from just that one find.

Quarrying was a merciless business. I'd spent a summer doing some for an uncle of mine. Because I was tall and muscular for my age he gave me the job of wielding a spalling hammer. The one I used went twelve pounds and was shaped something like a sledgehammer. If you weren't muscular before you started using a spalling hammer, you sure were by the end of the season.

About halfway through the summer, I was breaking rock with the big hammer when a piece of rock flew up and cut my right eye. At first they didn't think my sight would ever come back. I wore an eyepatch for eight months. The girls at the local barn dances liked it just fine.

"My farm's right behind that limestone cliff over there," Tucker said, using the stem of his pipe as a pointer. "So I couldn't really see much of the explosion. But I did see the three of them standing where we are right now. Grieves I'd seen in a saloon a few days ago. Hate to say it but he was kind of a loudmouth. Got into some pretty good arguments about the war with a pair of men we always consider kind of experts in the subject. Got so pissed off at one of them, he grabbed him by the front of the shirt and threw him back against the bar. That's when Gildy—Gildersleeve's his name—Gildy come runnin' around from behind the bar with this sawed-off and put it right in Grieves's face, see? And Gildy says I don't give a shit if you're a federal man or not, you don't come in here and start trouble with my regular customers."

"How'd Grieves take it?"

"Kinda surprised me for bein' such a loudmouth. He just said that he was sorry he got so carried away and that the drinks was on him."

"How long after that did you see him here with the girl and her uncle?"

He thought about it. "Day or two. More like two probably."

"But you didn't see how they caused the explosion to happen?"

"No sir, 'fraid I didn't. But when I heard it I dropped my plow and came runnin' up to the edge of the cliff and saw them over here."

"They see you?"

"Can't say for sure. But probably. Wasn't tryin' to hide or nothing."

"You hear any more explosions that day?"

"Nope. And I stayed in that part of the field till sundown. I woulda heard if there'd been one."

I had a full, good view of the quarry and an even better one with my field glasses.

I'd seen the recent gouge when we'd first gone up there. It was wide enough and deep enough that I didn't need the field glasses to see it. But then I did use them for close inspection.

"You're sure this is the only explosion there's been out here recently?"

"Positive, Mr. Ford. Nobody's worked this quarry for two years. Not since that hellish flood we had. This place was under water for six months. They had to set up a new quarry elsewhere."

"And they always used dynamite here?"

"Sure. Except for a certain kind of stone where they'd

use the old stuff, the gunpowder. There's a few jobs dynamite's too rough for."

I continued to scan. Usually around a quarry you see blasting caps from dynamite use. But the flood had cleaned out everything.

From what I could see, the large hole in the face of the cliff was just as Tucker had said. Brand new.

"Wish I could be more helpful, Mr. Ford. You know, seen what he was using to make the blast. But they run right down there and cleaned up the whole site. Like they didn't want to leave no kind of evidence behind."

Grieves had gotten his hands on something that was pretty damned dangerous. And would likely be worth a lot of money to somebody. If, that is, it was a grenade or grenade-like device that didn't kill the thrower as often as it killed the intended victims.

I couldn't gauge anything about the reliability of the weapon but I could certainly gauge its ferocity. What I'd just seen impressed me with not only the concussive power of the weapon but also the fact that its damage was much better focused than most grenades. You didn't get accuracy in grenades; this weapon looked as if you pretty much destroyed what you aimed at.

My thoughts went back to my own war, the bloody, busted bodies of my own time's battlefields. There were all kinds of diseases to conquer but the real money and real interest seemed to lie in destruction rather than preservation. I wasn't naïve enough to be a pacifist but I was realistic enough to know that something was wrong when nations spent more money on death than life.

I thanked Tucker for taking me up there and then I headed back to town.

I was in need of a cup of coffee so I strolled toward the café. The main street was still noisy and dusty with wagon traffic. A train coming into the depot added to the noise.

I had just passed the sheriff's office when Knut Jagland came out in a hurry and said, "We've been looking for you. We need to get over to the mortuary quick."

Within five minutes I was staring down at a corpse that was covered only by a sheet. The corpse had blue eyes. One of them was glass.

Chapter 17

"You gonna make a joke?"

"About what?"

"About how fast I got us out of that room downstairs?"

"Why would I make a joke?"

"I know you already figured that I hate bein' around blood. But bein' in a tiny room with a dead body, that makes me even sicker. It's like bein' in a coffin. Knut here's a big help to me."

"Hell, Sheriff, we're all afraid of something," Knut said. "Look at me and snakes."

Sheriff Terhurne nodded. "He's like a little girl around 'em."

The way Knut glanced at him, I wasn't sure he was all that happy with how Terhurne had explained Knut's aversion to snakes.

We stood in the backyard of the mortuary next to the double garage that held the fancy hearse and the bone wagon. There were nice big oaks for shade and if you didn't look at the Victorian-style house in back of you, you wouldn't know that you were within maybe thirty feet of dead folks.

"You looked like you knew him, Noah," Knut said.

"I don't know him but I'm pretty sure I know who he was."

"He got anything to do with Grieves?" Terhurne said.

"Yes. But I haven't quite figured out what yet." Then: "You two can head back to the office if you want. I'm going back downstairs."

Terhurne smiled. "You like those corpses, do you?"

I wasn't in the mood for his humor. Knut said, "C'mon, Sheriff, let's see what's at the office."

"I'm sorry if I offended you," Terhurne said to me. I thought of what they said about Germans, that they were always either at your throat or at your feet. Seems some Irishers had that same inclination. I didn't like Terhurne any better kissing my ass than threatening me.

❁

He hadn't been in the river long, Dobbs the scientist, not according to the mortuary man Sam Nevens, anyway.

Nevens wore an expensive white shirt, an expensive blue cravat, and obviously spent some time on his graying hair. He was the middle-aged mortician as fashion plate. He was all about life in his calling of death.

We both pushed cigarette smoke across the body between us on the table. Nevens had moved us into the preparation room with much larger space.

I was asking questions about how long the body had been in the water but he had a complaint to register first.

"You know something, Mr. Ford? I'm completely happy to answer your questions. In fact, I'll stand here all day and talk your leg off about how bodies respond to water. And you know what? There won't be any charge. And do you know how I know how bodies respond to water?"

"No, I guess I don't." I wondered where the hell this was going. The body had been washed up, not even the bullet holes in the side of the head looking all that foul at that point. But still and all it was a dead body and I didn't want to stay there any longer than I had to.

"Well, how I learned about bodies and water was when I went to school in Denver. Yes, mortician's school. People are all the time asking us questions but they never stop to think of where we learned the answers."

"Yeah, well, that's really too bad—but—"

"—and you know who makes the biggest profit in this business? Not us, that's for darned sure. You go right down the street to this big fancy furniture store, Clancy Brothers, and you think all you're seeing is the furniture they get in from Chicago five times a year. But then you go down in the basement and you know what you find?"

"Mr. Nevens, I'm in kind of a hurry—"

"Caskets is what you find. My pop who built this funeral home, he and the original Mr. Clancy got into an argument over pinochle one night. And damned if Clancy didn't go into the casket business two weeks later. A whole basement full of them. And for twenty years that's the way it's been. We do all the hard work here—did you happen to notice the new wallpaper in the vestibule upstairs?—and they make the easy money on caskets."

I was trapped in a room with a dead man and a lunatic.

He tried to keep on talking but I took out my railroad watch and dangled it in front of him. "I have five minutes to get to an important meeting."

"And what important meeting would that be?"

"That important meeting would be none of your damned business. Now tell me how long you think the body has been in the water."

"I was just trying to give you a little background is all. And in a very friendly way, if I may say so."

I'd hurt his feelings. I dropped my watch back into my pocket. "I appreciate that but I really am in a hurry."

"Well, all you had to do was say so." He pulled the sheet back from the corpse. "I'd say no longer than half a day to three-quarters of a day. And the reason I say that—"

"That's good enough. Now I have one more question. The fisherman who brought him in, where did he say he found him?"

"Drifting close to shore."

"I meant what area of the river did he find him in?"

"Up on the islet. Devon's Islet, they call it."

I put my hat on. "I appreciate it, Mr. Nevens."

"I'll be happy to walk you out—"

"I can find my way. Thanks. I appreciate your help."

When I was halfway up the stairs, he said, "My dream is to sell my own caskets someday and not have to deal with Clancy at all."

I shouted back down: "That's a dream we all share, Mr. Nevens."

Nan and Glen Turner's hotel had a nice coffee den that offered a good view of the stairs. I'd inquired if she and her husband were in and the clerk had obligingly told me they were. I decided to have a few cups of coffee and sort through some thoughts while I waited to see if they would do me the favor of leaving the hotel any time soon.

Somewhere was something that everybody seemed to want. Molly, Uncle Bob, Nan all seemed to think I had it or knew where it was, whatever it happened to be. I had the sense that Dobbs, the dead man with the blue glass eye, was the originator of it and that Grieves wanted to be a part of it, the "it" being the thing that would go "boom boom boom" and make the possessor a lot of money. We were likely dealing with government secrets here. Even, perhaps, treason.

And then there was Swarthout and Ella Coltrane. They didn't seem happy that I was looking into this at all. Maybe they already had whatever it was and were afraid I'd find that out.

And what did the sheriff know about it? A lot had happened in his town since Grieves and Dobbs had been there. A curious lawman would have to draw some kind of conclusions, wouldn't he? But then maybe Terhurne was so obsessed with winning reelection that he hadn't paid any attention to what was going on.

And then we were back to three murders. Uncle Bob, Molly, Dobbs. And Grieves missing and maybe murdered, too. Were they all related to whatever it was that a handful of people wanted so desperately?

About half an hour after I first put cup to lip, Nan and her husband appeared on the staircase, talking as they descended. Neither looked happy. Impossible to know if this was a battle over who had most recently violated a marriage vow or whether it had anything to do with the Grieves matter.

They didn't stop at the desk. Nan got the expected number of glances from gentlemen, one of whom she anointed with a smile.

Five minutes later, I walked to the double doors of

the hotel, looked both ways to make sure that neither of them was nearby, then went into the alley and entered the hotel from the back.

Room 19 was easy to find and easy to open thanks to the burglary tools I carried with me.

They had a large suite filled with pompous Victorian furnishings and enough geegaws and doodads, including a chandelier that could crush an elephant, to make the most pretentious New Orleans madam envious.

They had two trunks and three suitcases. I'd had serious experience riffling rooms and knew how to be both quick and careful. They had expensive clothes, at least half of which were scanty bedroom attire for Nan, and fancy ruffled shirts for hubby.

I was figuring on a sketchy search of the bedroom bureau that stood across from the massive canopy bed. There was enough perfume on the air to tear my eyes up.

You don't expect hotel guests to have brought enough material to pack drawers but these folks had. Twice I had to stop when I heard distant voices in the hall. The suite was so sizable and so filled with furnishings and thick rugs and thick wallpaper that most sounds from outside were cut off. It was like being inside a vault.

A lot of jewelry, though I suspected this was glass. The real stuff, if there was any, would be downstairs in the hotel safe.

What I wasn't looking for but was happy to find was a small box disguised as something fancy and fake-gold for milady.

Except for diplomats and assassins, I'd never known anybody who'd packed eight different passports before. Sixteen altogether for the Mr. and Mrs. There were the expected ones of the U.S., Britain, France, Germany, and Italy but also South Africa and two Caribbean countries.

And then it came together. I still didn't know what "it" was but I could see where the players fit. Nan and Glen dealt with scientists who could be blackmailed or bought off. Scientists would give them samples and plans for a highly secret weapon they were working on. And Nan and Glen would give them money. Or promise to destroy the blackmail material. D.C. probably had a thick file on them. Maybe a couple of thick files. They were the ultimate opportunists. And all across the world. You never knew what little country was going to come up with the rudiments of a super weapon. And there would be a long line of folks to obtain them, with an eye to selling the "it" to a larger country for many, many times more than they'd paid for "it."

I took the passports, shoved them in my back pocket, and finished going through the rest of the drawers. Nothing useful turned up.

I was just about to leave the bedroom when I heard the door open in the living room and Nan say, "I still don't like the way Sheriff Terhune kept looking at us. Like he knows something about us."

"He's just some hayseed. He doesn't know anything." Then he laughed. "You were at your worst in that haberdasher's, by the way. You're always bitching about how I embarrass you. How about how you embarrass me?"

"Why didn't you take her out in the alley and attack her? I'm pretty sure she would've liked it, the way you two were making eyes at each other."

"For God's sake, Nan, all she was doing was selling me a couple of shirts. She's probably got three kids at home and sings in the church choir every Sunday."

"Isn't that what you prefer? Remember when we first met and you said you liked the 'unlikely' ones best?"

"That was twelve years ago. Now let me throw these shirts on the table here and we'll go down and have a couple of drinks."

"Maybe the shop woman'll be down there waiting for you."

They were making a pretty good argument against marriage. At least for people like them.

"Maybe I'll just stay up here."

"Oh, don't go in for one of your sulks. If anybody should be sulking it's me. I still think you hooked up with that federal man the other night."

"At least he bathes."

"I don't know why you keep bringing up that girl in Cheyenne. I've apologized every chance I've had. And she did bathe. You were just making that up to hurt me."

"The hell I was. You stank like a cesspool when you slipped into bed that night." Then: "Now hurry up and let's go downstairs. Now that you brought up that stinky bitch in Cheyenne, I need a drink."

"I wish you hadn't brought up that sheriff. Now you've got me worrying about him, too. Maybe he's not as dumb as he looks."

"Nobody could be."

I'd been ready to move but now I didn't have to. The front door closed. I heard them walk away but the hall carpeting soon absorbed their footsteps.

I took one more turn around the bedroom, making sure I hadn't missed another suitcase.

The extra turn was worth the time it took. I found a calendar with the next day's date circled. I also found a file with three articles about Dr. Nathan Dobbs. The articles were dated two years earlier. They referenced his expertise with hand-carried weapons for foot soldiers. There was even a photograph that displayed his glass eye perfectly. And there was a postcard from Dobbs, simply stating that he would be in Junction City on a certain date, which was three weeks earlier.

Had they met up?

Chapter 18

Knut stopped me halfway to the livery. "There's gonna be a town council meeting tonight about the sheriff. This is something that just sorta happened on its own. There's enough steam in this town right now that it's going to take place even if Swarthout or anybody tries to block it. They say it's gonna be a kind of referendum on how Sheriff Terhurne runs this office."

"One of his opponents probably drummed this up."

"Absolutely." He paused. "He asked me if I'd ask you to do him a favor."

"Aw, shit."

"You wouldn't have to say much, Noah. Just that things sorta happen sometimes and that Terhurne has fired Hayden for dereliction of duty and that as far as you can tell, Terhurne is a pretty good sheriff."

"I get paid for this?"

He didn't smile. He looked, in fact, sort of amazed.

"I was kidding, Knut."

The smile came wide then.

"You got to remember I'm not used to big-city humor. And you seem like such an honest person, I was really surprised."

"Well, I guess I can do that but I don't see that it'll

matter much. Federal men aren't all that popular. In case you hadn't noticed."

"Well, he'd appreciate you givin' it a try. Six-thirty in the little building next to the post office. Thanks, Noah."

❖

Twenty minutes later I was on my horse. I rode out to where Dobbs's body had been found.

I was grateful to be back outdoors and alone. The snow on the mountain peaks, the green of the pines on the low hills, the smell of river and grass soothed me.

The islet turned out to be nothing more than a spit of sand with a few tangles of weeds to give it a more solid look than it deserved. It must have been underwater at least three or four times a year. This was where Dobbs's body had washed up.

I spent half an hour working that spit. Aside from a few pieces of branches, a couple of rusty tin cans, an ancient shoe that various animals had taken turns gnawing on, there wasn't much to see.

A couple of times I knelt next to the water and dragged my hands through it to see if I could find anything that the lawmen might have overlooked. All I got was some oily residue. There must have been a factory on the river somewhere nearby, I thought. This was a political battle in many territories. Industry was all well and good but there were problems with it that nobody had foreseen.

I went back to my horse and took my field glasses from my saddlebag.

Far in the distance I could see the unused railroad tracks shining. These would lead to the resort. I was tempted to follow them but it was late in the day by then.

I mounted up and started back, disappointed that nothing had turned up where the fisherman had found the body.

On the way back to town I glimpsed the mansion that Swarthout had let Grieves use. I eased on over there.

It was antebellum by way of Colonial. Sitting on an unending sea of green grass, properly kept to the blade, it had the sort of storybook appeal that Molly Kincaid would have loved. Inside you'd expect to find Cinderella or at least a princess or two.

The sun had started to turn bloody and the blood shone on the numerous windows of the place. The bird feeders were busy with at least a dozen kinds of birds. The gazebo was big enough for a hoedown.

I dismounted and just stood there, taking in the sounds and scents of the dying day.

I walked the grounds. The plot was extensive, leading to two massive garages in the rear. The property at the back was defined by an endless line of forest.

I walked around inside the barn and stables. No animals and the turds I found were hard and dry.

A crow sat on a wagon watching me. There was something spectral about him, like a portent of monstrous deeds. Very different feel to the back of the place—one of desertion, I guess, as if something terrible had passed through there and would soon pass through again—and so I headed back to the front.

I went up the front steps, used my reliable burglary tools, and opened the massive double doors with their intricate carvings and enormous brass fittings. Gargoyles peered at me from both doors.

Inside, my steps began to echo. The dying day darkened the huge vestibule in which I stood. Empty and dark, it had the feeling of a cathedral that God had fled. Or maybe my definition of God was wrong. Maybe the people who'd come here had a different kind of God than mine. They worshipped money. I remembered once seeing a man in expensive shoes slapping the head of the shoeshine boy who was working on his shoes. The boy was doing a fine job but not fine enough for the man in the top hat and enormous cigar. I needed my own boots shined and was waiting my turn. But the harder the man slapped the boy on the head, the less I could control myself, until finally I lunged at the man, grabbed the hand he was slapping with, and hurled him down to the floor. I made him tip the boy ten times what he normally would and then I chased his ass out the door. I imagined that this mansion had been filled with men like him.

I walked deeper inside. I stood beneath a chandelier wide enough to cover the ceilings of most of the rooms I stayed in. From here I saw the outline of the grand staircase that twisted and turned upward into a darkness that brought back the image of the crow and the secrets in his fierce dark unknowable eyes.

I stood still for long moments, listening. Wind in trees; spring limbs scraping windows; one of the outbuilding doors banging in the wind; creaks and ghostly groans of the house.

I found a candle and lighted it and then walked around the ground floor. A grand piano dominated the living room. The couches and divans were in the current English style, spare and uncomfortable looking. The den was packed with books, maps, an enormous globe, and an open space that might be used for a string quartet. You could roast a couple of cows in the fireplace. A fancy French restaurateur would have envied the enormous stoves, ovens, cabinetry, chopping blocks, and jungle of pots and pans hanging from a device suspended from the ceiling. Two long windows looked out upon a section of lawn where croquet pieces stood

in place, awaiting players. Easy to imagine smartly
dressed men and women on a mild June Sunday playing
the game and laughing oh so civilly when one of them
missed a shot.

The upstairs was as lavish as the downstairs. Four
bedrooms, two of them suites, each furnished in taste
more French than British and a hell of a lot more comfortable looking.

I was back to looking through drawers again. Nothing.
Nor in the closets. Grieves might have stayed there for
some time but he certainly didn't leave anything behind.

I started to leave the largest of the bedrooms when
my eyes went to a wastebasket by a small desk. I didn't
find anything in that one but I decided to check back
through all the wastebaskets in the house.

And in the den downstairs, shoved under the opening in the massive desk, I found the wastebasket that
yielded a partially written letter.

Star Commercial Lines
14387 Addison Street
San Francisco, California

Dear Sir,
*I shall require a first class compartment on a ship
leaving for Argentina on June 28*

Here the ink smudged and that was when he'd balled
up the paper and fired it into the wastebasket.

I'd never seen an example of Grieves's writing before
but I was assuming this was his letter.

I had two thoughts almost simultaneously. One, that
he was asking for one ticket. Two, that his partner
Dobbs had been hauled from the river with a pair of
bullets in his head.

Traveling light. Whatever "it" was, and it likely had to be one of the hand-carried weapons referred to in the articles I'd seen, Grieves had decided to keep the money for himself when Nan and Glen bought the material from him.

I smoothed out the letter, folded it small, and then headed back to town.

Chapter 19

It wasn't as much a town meeting as a prelude to a lynching.

There was a desk in front and maybe twenty chairs for the fifty or so people who had crowded in the small, narrow room that had been sloppily painted lime green and hung with photographs of territorial bigwigs, one of whom looked familiar to me. I sat in one of the two chairs facing the crowd. Sheriff Terhurne sat in the other.

"You been at this job too long."

"It's an embarrassment, havin' a prisoner killed like that."

"If you were the right kind, you'd hand in your badge, somethin' like this happening."

Easy to see that these were the minions of one Sy Compkins Rafferty, the tall, woodsman-like man who stood in the back of the room with his arms folded and a smirk on his carefully mustached face. He was enjoying seeing the opposition wince and stammer and flounder every time was asked a question.

Much as I didn't want to, I felt sorry for Terhurne. Nobody in the law enforcement business is without flaw. For all his arrogance, he seemed a reasonably competent sheriff to me.

On a soft spring night like that one, people should have been out for a stroll, not packed into that mean little room watching a man like Terhurne humiliated.

Rafferty, I assumed, was hoping that Terhurne would be forced to resign on the spot. Or to say something so arrogant or stupid that Rafferty would win the election.

He'd prepared them well. A full hour went by. Terhurne looked more and more beleaguered until he finally said, somewhat pathetically, "I saved your dog from drowning, Mrs. Whitman, don't that mean anything?"

"Saved a dog from drowning!" somebody laughed. "He's a regular good Samaritan."

An elderly man stood up and said, "I think we owe you an apology for this evening, Sheriff. Rafferty back there put a lot of people up to makin' fun of you tonight. But I just come because I think maybe it's time we had ourselves a new sheriff, that's all. I think you done a real good job, Sheriff Terhurne, but with this young gal getting killed right in the jail and your nephew—Well, four, five years ago you wouldn't have hired your nephew. You woulda been smarter than that. It's a matter of judgment. Any time a man hires a relative in a public position like you got—well, that's just askin' for trouble." His arthritic hands came together almost in prayer. "So what I'm proposing here—and I don't give a hang if Rafferty likes it or not—is that the town council gives you a bonus of $500 and then gives a monthly stipend for your retirement. This town owes you a lot—" He turned then and cast a scolding eye on his fellow townsmen. Even Rafferty looked embarrassed by the trick he'd tried to pull there at that gathering. "And I plan to bring it up tomorrow at the official town council meeting."

Whoever the old man was, he was three times as smart and four times as articulate as most of the pompous bastards in the national Congress. And he obviously had an effect on his fellows. Man and woman alike looked chastened by his words. A man sitting in front of Rafferty spoke up and said, "That's a very wise speech you give, Nick. And I'm all for it."

Before the crowd could stand up and make it unanimous, I stood up and faced them.

Rafferty, sensing what might be coming said, "You don't have no say in this, federal man. Sit down. We all know you threw in with Terhurne here."

"I didn't throw in with anybody. I'm just doing my job. And Terhurne is helping me."

Terhurne said: "Folks, I admit that I'm responsible for what happened in my own jail. And I know I need help to find out who killed Molly Kincaid. I know you think I'm arrogant sometimes—and sometimes I guess I am—but I'm not so arrogant that I don't know a superior lawman when I see one. And that's why I'm happy that Mr. Ford here is in charge of the investigation. I'm doing all I can to help him."

Rafferty: "I wouldn't need no help if I was runnin' this investigation. I'd have the killer in jail or strung up by now."

A few followers remained loyal and made some minor noises in Rafferty's favor. But most seemed to see that even if they didn't like Terhurne, he was asking for their sympathy and help. Apparently just admitting that he'd made a mistake was enough to shock most people at the meeting that night.

I said: "There's an election coming up, folks. And I'm assuming there'll be a couple of debates between the candidates. That's the time to decide who you want to vote for. And I'd ask you to consider their histories and experience. Terhurne isn't young anymore but from what I can see he's got a very good deputy in Knut Jagland. And Knut's getting a good grounding in law enforcement from Terhurne. I'd keep those things in mind."

Rafferty: "I thought you weren't takin' any sides in this?"

"I'm not much for lynch mobs, Rafferty. And I don't appreciate the way you called for this meeting tonight. You just wanted to embarrass Terhurne and nothing else. I don't think that's a good start for a man who wants to be a lawman. Stirring people up is always dangerous, no matter who does it."

I glimpsed Liz Thayer sticking her head in the door, notebook and pencil in hand. She must have been covering things from the hall. No room to squeeze in. She'd want a dramatic finish for the evening but she wasn't getting one. Nobody stood up and speechified. Reasonable people are usually quiet people. Terhurne hadn't converted them back to his side. But I think they'd had a close look at Rafferty and now had doubts about him as anything more than a mouth without a brain.

Nobody said goodnight. Nobody came up to offer a hand. Nobody even nodded at us. They just filed silently out the door. Rafferty had disappeared.

Liz came into the room and walked up to us. "Going to be a close election, Sheriff."

"I wonder if I even want it anymore."

"Sure you do. Or your pride does, anyway. You might quit after you win. But you want to win first."

"Damned pride," Terhurne said. "And nobody's got more pride than a mick like me."

"Rafferty makes you look like a great statesman," I said. "He's doing you a favor by being in the race."

"Where's Knut tonight?" Liz asked.

Terhurne nodded to me. "Noah here thought it'd be good to make Knut night sheriff. Not have a kid at night. But a real sheriff. That's his title now. Night sheriff."

That had been the only way I could see to bring the younger, smarter Knut into prominence without damaging Terhurne any more than I had to. Day sheriff and night sheriff. It had worked for a while in Kansas City. No reason it wouldn't work in Junction City.

"I've got to get back to the newspaper. You going back to your hotel, Noah?"

"Be my pleasure to escort such a fine-looking lady."

Terhurne smiled. "I used to talk fancy like that. But it doesn't work when you're old. You just look silly."

"Well, for what it's worth, Terhurne, she's always telling me how old I am."

He studied me. "Well, I think she might have a point there."

Liz laughed but I wasn't so sure he was kidding.

❄

"You know, he really shouldn't be reelected," Liz said as we walked down the street.

"I know. But look at who's running against him."

"That's always been his saving grace. He's never had any real competition." Then: "God, wish I could put this night in a bottle and keep it with me all the time. Smell the apple blossoms. But you have to go back to your stuffy little hotel room and I have to go back to my newspaper."

"We could always have a meal and talk."

"You know what that means, Noah, and I don't want to hurt your feelings."

"Too old, eh?"

"You know it's not just that. I just can't do things that way. Soon as you figure out what's going on here, you'll be gone. Then I'd be left feeling sort of—loose. I don't like feeling that way about myself. A lot of the town women are already suspicious of me. Now that I'm divorced they think I've got my eyes on their husbands. I don't want to give them the wrong impression by being loose."

"Well, I guess that's the way it'll have to be."

When she hugged me, the top of her head came right to the middle of my chest. Her breasts, her warmth, and woman scent of her made me lonelier than I cared to feel so I pushed her gently away.

"I'm kind of restless, I guess," I said. "Think I'll go have a cup of coffee and a piece of pie."

"Thanks for understanding, Noah."

She went inside the lighted newspaper office. Somebody was using the press. Looked like the same man I'd seen there earlier.

I wanted coffee but I also wanted a walk. Liz hadn't been kidding about bottling that night. It was one of the soft warm nights when you'd sleep with the window cracked open and you'd feel good about things in a way you hadn't for a long time. One of God's small but indispensable blessings. Especially those apple blossoms.

I ended up downline from the depot where the railroad line kept a large garage for repairs. The smell of engine oil brought back boyhood. I'd been around the big trains long before they'd been able to call themselves transcontinental. I'd doted on trains the way other boys doted on hitting home runs. Trains were magical.

A small diner. A horse at the hitching post. The aroma of strong coffee and some kind of pie, probably apple.

The only other customer was a geezer at the end of the counter. He had set his teeth out next to his coffee cup and was pulling his mouth back into fake smiles. The storeboughts must have been giving him some pain. Old age sure didn't look all that appealing.

A wiry bald man took my order and laid out my coffee and pie within a minute of my planting my ass on the counter stool.

Just after he set my coffee down, he glanced over my shoulder to the window. He must have seen something out there because his expression got tight and nervous.

He leaned in so Toothless down the way couldn't hear. "I ain't getting involved in this but there's a couple fellas out there that I'm pretty sure are waitin' for you."

"You know them?"

"Like I said, I don't want to get involved."

The counterman went away. Toothless put his teeth back in, tossed some money on the counter, and left.

The counterman stayed away from me. I glanced over my shoulder only once. I got a ghostlike glimpse of a large man peering out from behind a tree to see if I was still in there. Another man peeked out moments later. They both wore the latest in bandana fashion for stagecoach robbers. Even in a glance one of the face-covering bandanas looked crusted with something. I didn't like to speculate on just what that might be.

For the time, I was safe where I was. But I didn't plan to be for long.

To the counterman, I said: "There a back door?"

"Please don't get me involved, mister. I got a sick wife."

"All I asked was if you had a back door?"

"Yeah, but I should tell you it sticks pretty bad. Don't tell 'em I told you that."

I decided to make them wait a while. I read a page of a very old newspaper. I drank a second cup of coffee. And then I strolled over to pay my bill. You always want the person you're watching to do something interesting. I made sure not to do a single thing interesting.

I would have to move fast. I drew my Colt and then made quickly for the back door to the right of the stove.

I could have run but I wanted to find out who they were working for. I had enough enemies in this town to be curious.

The counterman hadn't been kidding about the door sticking. The kitchen had been scrubbed down and cleaned up for the night. Everything looked orderly. Except the door. You could see where weather had warped it along the edge and that it bloated out enough that it didn't quite fit into the frame in places.

All this gave the thugs watching me the impression that I was going to run out the back door. I hoped they'd be tricked.

I managed to get the door kicked open and then I turned around and headed out the front way. By now the thug I'd seen running from the tree would be waiting for me in the back.

I stood just at the edge of the front of the building. He came racing around from the back. Running, he was off balance. All I needed to do was kick his legs out from under him.

He was a heavyset man in a red plaid shirt and dungarees. In the moonlight his bandana looked blue. His black wide-brimmed hat flew off when he slammed face first into the ground.

He hit hard enough that he let go of the club he'd been carrying. But the other hand still clutched the six-shooter. That was easily enough taken care of. Before he could even think of using it, I walked over and brought the heel of my boot down hard right on his knuckles. He lost his grip. I kicked his gun into the darkness.

He expressed his pain in curses. He knew some good ones. He'd been going to use his club on me, if not his gun. I didn't owe him being gentle. I kicked him hard in the ribs.

His mask started to slip and he grabbed it with his good hand, pulled it all the way up to his eyes.

"Get up."

He kept his face flat to the ground. He didn't want me to see it. He didn't look in any way familiar.

Curious then, I reached down and started to grab his mask. I was still aware that there was another punk lurking around somewhere.

That was when I heard the footsteps. Only afterward did I realize that whoever it was wanted me to hear the footsteps. He wanted me standing up so he could aim true.

And true it was. He threw a sizable rock at me. The force knocked me to the ground. He wasn't finished. He must have realized how much he'd hurt me. All it took was one solid punch and I fell flat on the ground.

All I had time to see was a second at most of the masked thug grappling to his feet.

The one standing above me said: "You stay out of our business in town here."

If either of them put more pain on me, I wasn't conscious to hear it or feel it.

I was long gone.

Chapter 20

"And here I thought you were a tough hombre."

The voice, female, was familiar. But who did it belong to?

"He got hit pretty hard, he did."

"Yeah, but he's federal. They're supposed to be tougher than the rest of us."

Whoever she was, her preferred means of communication was sarcasm.

I was struggling to get my eyes open. Having difficulty. And even when I did manage to get one of them open everything was so fuzzy I still couldn't tell who was talking.

"I guess I'll just have to write an editorial about how federal men just aren't as tough as we'd thought."

The diminutive Liz Thayer. Frontier journalist.

The scents then. Medical scents.

I was on an examining table.

The doc, who was a fleshy middle-aged man with thinning red hair, was presently putting a wooden stethoscope to my chest.

"His heart seems to be all right."

"I'm surprised he's got a heart."

The doc laughed. "You're a mean one, you are."

Now both eyes were open. Liz leaned in and said, "I was just kidding you so you'd wake up faster. Getting mad gives you energy."

"That's her idea of medicine," the doc said.

"I was walking home from the newspaper when a man came running up the street shouting. He took me over to you. We got you up on a horse and brought you over here. Which reminds me, I stole somebody's horse. I'd better be getting it back."

"I thank you for that."

"Any idea of who did this to you, Noah?"

"The first one had a mask on. The second one I didn't see at all."

I made the mistake of trying to raise my head just a bit. The pain in my skull traveled all the way down into my shoulders. I heard myself groan.

"Probably not a good idea," the doc said. "I'd just stay still."

"I need to get back to my room. I've got things to do early tomorrow morning."

"Not right away you don't. I need you to lie here for an hour. I think you can probably manage that, can't you?" Then: "Damned patients. You try to help them and they fight you all the way."

"We heard you, Doc," Liz said.

"Good. I meant you to." He walked to the door. "Now you sit here and entertain him. I've got things to do in my little lab. I'll be back in an hour."

When he left, Liz said, "I'm going to find out who they were."

"Who who were?"

"The two that did this to you."

"I pretty much know they came from Rafferty."

"I know. But I want you to know which two it was."

"You got a stake in this?"

"Yes. If they're who I think they are, they're two men who need to get slapped around for a good long time. And you can do it."

"You read too many dime novels. I'm no hero. Two men at one time. They'd put me right back here."

"No, dopey. You'd go after them one at a time. You're not thinking clearly."

"Right now the last thing I want to think about is fighting."

I closed my eyes.

"I don't think you're supposed to do that."

"Why not?"

"I don't remember. But I read it somewhere. About when you suspect somebody's got a concussion."

"The doc didn't say anything about that."

"He probably forgot. I got him rattled. He thinks I talk too much."

"I sure can't imagine where he'd get an idea like that."

"Very funny."

At some point in the narrow silence that ensued I fell deep down into the welcome crevice of sleep. Luxurious, healing sleep.

Then: "So what's so important about tomorrow morning?"

I woke again. "What?"

"I said what's so important about tomorrow morning?"

"I can't tell you."

"Must be federal, huh?"

"Very federal."

"I talk too much but I'm good at keeping secrets."

"Good for you. I still can't tell you."

"You've figured something out, haven't you?"

"Maybe."

"The payoff?"

Her words startled me. I started to raise my head but then groaned and laid it back down again.

"You shouldn't try and sit up, Noah."

"Thanks for the advice. And what the hell do you know about the 'payoff,' as you call it?"

"I'm a newspaper woman, remember? Meaning I'm not stupid. Meaning I've thought a lot about what's going on in this town. Meaning that Grieves and Dobbs got together. Dobbs had something secret he wanted to sell. Given the articles I read about him, he was obviously selling something the government considers secret. Dobbs wouldn't know how to market it but Grieves would. Those were my first thoughts. Want to hear a few more?"

"I'm just going to lie here and pretend I'm dead. I'm not hearing anything you're saying."

"That's because I've figured it out and federal men don't want newspaper women to figure anything out. It threatens them. If a dumb little newspaper woman can figure it out, then maybe my job isn't so tough after all. Maybe I'm not the big shot I think I am."

"I'm not hearing any of this, remember? I'm officially dead."

"So anyway, I'm trying to figure out who Grieves would be dealing with in town here. And when you analyze it, there are only two people it could be. And that would be Nan and Glen Turner. They've got connections somewhere. Probably everywhere. They pay Grieves and Dobbs so much money for the whatever it is and then they re-sell it for a lot more money somewhere else. Pretty good so far, isn't it?"

"I know where this is leading and you're not going with me."

"Sure I am. And you can't stop me. I may not be riding alongside you but I'll be behind you somewhere."

"Grieves is a killer, Liz. You know that already."

She leaned over and kissed me on the forehead. "Well you may not have noticed, old man, but so am I. And if things get rough, I'll be there to protect you." Then: "I just wish you weren't too old for me."

Chapter 21

Just before midnight, the doc came in, checked me over, and said I could leave on my own.

"You're doing a lot better than I would have thought."

"Glad you think so, anyway."

"She's somethin', ain't she? Liz, I mean."

"Sure is."

"That first husband of hers, he didn't deserve her."

As we talked, he helped me to my feet. Dizziness and shaky knees made me wonder if the doc knew what the hell he was talking about. But after a minute or so the worst of the dizziness passed and my knees stopped trembling.

"I heard what she said about you being too old."

"Thin walls, huh?"

"She's all romantic about handsome young men."

We reached the darkness of the outer office.

"Walk over to the front door now."

I did so with no problem. "Look good to me."

"How much I owe you, Doc?"

"Two dollars."

"Fair enough."

I walked back and put the money on his desk.

"I also heard you two talking about starting out early in the morning."

"You heard some dangerous things, Doc. You shouldn't've been listening."

"At my age, what else I got to do?" His cranky smile was luminous in the shadows of the office. "And you don't need to be worryin' about me tellin' anybody else, either."

"Good. Because if you did tell somebody what I'm going to do, I'd come back here and show you how unhappy I was."

"Not much for threats."

"Neither am I. Givin' or takin' 'em. But I expect you to keep quiet."

"This conversation sure got crazy fast. All I meant when I brought up tomorrow morning was that you'll have to take it awful easy."

"Fine. That's what I'll do."

"Somehow I don't believe you but it's up to you. It's your life."

The night air revived me further. The head still ached but it was down a few notches and I had my mind on things other than the pain.

The occasional lamplight lent the sleepy town a kind of storybook aspect. So neat and clean, all its physical sins hidden by the shadows. A few chimneys plumed smoke into the starry sky, here and there a lamp burned, maybe a book reader or a parent worried about a child with fever.

I'm pretty sure I was asleep by the time I got back to my room.

❂

My body just plain didn't want to get up. A good washing, three cups of coffee, a chilly breeze through the open window, and the damned thing still wanted to head right back to the bed to hide under the covers for another eight or nine days. My mind kept trying to give it orders. But all the body did was make a dirty gesture.

But I had no choice. I had to get up, to function and function reasonably well. If my calculation was right about the date circled on Nan's calendar, this was an important day.

Liz waited for me at the restaurant. She patted an empty chair as if I was her pet dog. I sat down where my master indicated.

"You look pretty rough, Noah."

"Thank you."

"How's your head?"

"Still attached to my shoulders."

"You're really in a terrible mood, aren't you?"

"Gosh, I can't imagine why."

The woman came for my order. Before my mind could even form the images of the breakfast I wanted, Liz said, "He'll have what I had, Mae."

"Thanks, Liz."

I looked at her plate.

All that was left were a few traces of gravy.

"Thanks for ordering for me."

"God, are you crabby. I thought I was doing you a favor."

"I can order my own breakfast. I'm a big boy."

"You don't sound like a big boy. You sound like a very spoiled small boy. I try and do you a favor and you go all sullen on me."

I drank my coffee. With the three I'd had at the hotel, I was starting to get those morning jitters that often accompany too much caffeine.

"I brought my carbine. I'm going to prove to you that I'm a good shooter, Noah."

"I still wish you weren't going."

"Please. Let's not go through this again."

I ate. She watched me. The head wound started to leak a little. She daubed at it with a clean white handkerchief. "I figured you'd still be bleeding. I also figured I'd have to take care of you."

By now, the town's most important people had started to gather in the room. Most of them glanced in my direction. None of them looked happy to see me.

"Sometimes I want to leave this town."

My mouth packed with eggs, potatoes, and coffee, responding to her was impossible. I shrugged.

"You probably don't believe that, do you?"

I just wanted to sit here and eat. I didn't want to hear about her life. I didn't care about her life. I shrugged silently again.

"But my folks helped settle this land here and that's sort of my heritage. Or does that sound corny?"

Another shrug.

"You have very expressive shoulders." She laughed. "You have a dab of egg yolk on your nose."

She found her trusty handkerchief again and cleaned off my face.

I finished up and said, "You really do talk a lot." Then: "There they are."

I'd stationed myself so that I had a clear view of the hotel where Nan and Glen had been staying. They wore riding clothes. Glen carried a Winchester. They'd be headed to the livery. I wasn't sure where they were going but I assumed they wouldn't be walking.

"He has a Winchester."

"I noticed that."

"I'll bet I'm a better shot than he is."

I glanced at her and smiled. "I'm afraid, my dear, that isn't saying much."

If there's a heaven, I sure hope it looks a lot like the territory we traveled through that day. The black oak and silver pine, Joshua and incense cedar, the shining river that curled around prehistoric abutments of rock packed with centuries-old limber pine that at least four Indian tribes held to be sacred. We didn't talk much because the beauty all around us required silence and reverence.

You could see why they'd built a resort out there. The loamy aromas alone had an almost narcotic effect on your senses. And the wind off the wide blue river was like a baptism, it birthed you anew in its purity.

One time I even caught Liz tearing up. I liked to think that maybe it was because of the sheer startling power of the land all around us.

But later I had to think again when she said, for no seeming reason: "He always said we'd live in a place like this someday."

"Who said?"

"My husband."

I think that was the first time I sensed real grief and loss in her. She'd always sort of kidded about her feelings toward the man before. But those words were pure pain. Those words spoke of a love still very much with her. I still wanted to sleep with her but now I wanted to help her some, too.

"Maybe he'll come back someday."

"If he does, I'll shoot him."

"You're one dangerous lady."

"Just shut up, Noah. Just shut up."

I smiled at her and rode on ahead a while. Give her some alone time.

✦

During my Pinkerton years I worked mostly out of Chicago, Baltimore, and Kansas City. There was a lot of surveillance work. A lot of agents will tell you that it's easy work. You just follow somebody around and jot down where he's gone and who he's seen. Better than being shot at, they'll tell you.

But it's boring. Your feet ache, you have to be extremely conscious of what the man you're following might do suddenly—like turn around and point at you and shout that you're following him—and only about 40 percent of the time does it yield anything interesting either to the party that engages the Pinks or to you as an agent.

Following somebody on horseback isn't a hell of lot more thrilling. You're doing the same thing except you're sitting atop an animal that is a virtual shitting machine. On a nice day, like this one was, the scenery provides the only real diversion.

I doubted that Nan and Glen Turner were going to spot us. From what I could see with my field glasses, they were too busy bickering to notice much else going on. One of them had undoubtedly slept with a stranger the night before and was now engaged in defending him or herself.

Liz said, "How come you keep looking back like that?"

"Because somebody's following us."

"Really?"

"Really."

"You know who?"

"Not yet."

"We're following somebody and somebody's following us?"

"Sure seems to be that way."

"Does stuff like this happen to you very often?"

"All the time."

"What're you going to do about it?"

"Nothing."

"Why not?"

"No reason to. I want to find out who they are and why they're following us. Give it some more time."

"Boy, I don't like this. They could ambush us or something."

"Just relax."

"They probably have guns."

"They probably do."

We rode side by side. I reached over and touched her arm. "If you'll take some advice from a creaky old man, we have guns, too."

She said, "Now let's be fair here, Noah. I never said you were creaky."

"I just put that part in so you'd feel sorry for me."

"Well, it didn't work."

After that, I didn't say anything for a long time.

Early in the afternoon, we stopped to water the horses and to feed ourselves with the beef and bread Liz had brought along.

We sat on the riverbank and she said, "You worried about who's following us?"

"I'm curious. Not worried."

"I just don't like the idea that somebody's behind us and we don't know who it is."

"I've got a pretty good idea of who it is."

"You do? Then why didn't you tell me?"

"I thought I'd wait till I got a look at him so I could be sure."

"Well, tell me who you think it is."

"Grab my field glasses and climb that tree over there and find out for yourself. You good at climbing trees?"

"I grew up with three brothers and I could outclimb every one of them."

"Well, we just came up from a pretty deep valley. You should be able to see him pretty easy."

She didn't even finish her sandwich. She went over to my saddlebags, snatched up the field glasses, and confronted the sizable oak.

She scrambled up it a hell of a lot faster than I could have even as a boy. When she got near the top, she called back, "I told you I was good at this."

"We'll have a ceremony back in town."

"You're just jealous."

And then she went about her business.

Didn't take her long. "Damn. I see him."

"Good."

"Let's see if you guessed right. Who is it?"

"Sheriff Terhurne."

"You're right. How'd you know?"

"Because there's an election coming up and he probably thinks that if he helps bring Grieves in, the voters'll put him back in office."

"He's finished."

"You know he's finished and I know he's finished but I'm not sure he knows he's finished."

She came back to the riverbank, sat down next to me, and resumed finishing off her beef sandwich.

"I sort of feel sorry for him."

"I don't," I said.

"You stuck up for him."

"I stuck up for him because I didn't like what Rafferty was doing."

"Oh. I wonder what he'll do after he loses. He never has any money. He owes quite a bit to Swarthout's bank, in fact."

"He's a big boy. He can figure it out."

"You're kind've cold right now, Noah."

"I just don't like him grandstanding. He obviously kept his eye on me, otherwise he wouldn't have known what we're up to."

"Imagine that," she said, "you spy on people all the time but when they spy on you, you don't like it at all."

"Yeah," I said, "imagine that."

Chapter 22

After a few more miles, and after Liz said we were obviously headed for the resort, I said, "There's a hollow back there just right for stopping Terhurne. We'll hide our horses in those trees over there and then wait for him."

"I wish I didn't feel sorry for him."

"I wish you didn't, either. If he hadn't had his nephew on duty that night, Molly would still be alive."

"You liked her, didn't you?"

"I don't know what I felt about her. But I didn't want to see her die. Maybe she could have found a decent life for herself after all this."

"People don't change, Noah."

"That's a myth," I said. "People change all the time. It's just that the people around them refuse to believe it."

Long shadows kept us well hidden. Terhurne wouldn't see us until it was too late. The spring warmth was turning chilly on us. By Liz's estimate, we had about an hour till we reached the resort. We should still have some daylight to see how we were going to approach the place. Grieves was a professional. He'd probably hired a few guns so he could meet any kind of surprise that came his way.

Nan and Glen Turner had apparently been pretty fortunate in their dealings with rogue scientists and federal people. They'd gotten the merchandise they'd wanted and they'd sold it for the price they'd wanted and they were still walking topside up here on earth. I guessed that they hadn't ever run into anybody like Grieves before.

Or maybe I was wrong. Maybe they'd run into a dozen Grieveses in their time. But maybe they were so treacherous themselves that they'd killed everybody they'd ever done business with. Just because Glen was a drunk and a dandy didn't mean he wasn't a killer when he needed to be. And I had no doubt that Nan could do what she needed to.

An owl shared his dirge with us.

He was riding faster than he had been, Terhurne was. Maybe with daylight starting to fade he realized that he needed to draw close to us so that we could all reach the resort at about the same time.

I had to judge his distance by the sound. When I figured he was far enough away that he wouldn't run over me, I came out from behind the copse of lodgepole pines and stood in the center of the trail. He stopped about ten feet away. He automatically dropped hand to gun but by then I had a Winchester on him.

"I don't remember asking for help."

"I don't remember needing to ask your permission to take my horse for a little ride, Ford."

"Drop the gun on the ground and then dismount easy."

"This is bullshit."

"That's right, it is. You shouldn't have been following me. Now do what I said."

He took his time. By then Liz stood next to me. She

whispered, "You wouldn't actually shoot him, would you?"

I grimaced. "You think we could talk about this later?"

He walked the distance between us. He didn't put his arms in the air. Embarrassing enough that I'd ambushed him that way.

He shook his head at Liz. "I don't want any mention of this in the paper."

I didn't let her answer. "How long have you been watching me?"

He shrugged. "Had Spoon do it."

"Who the hell is Spoon?"

"That's his cousin's kid," Liz said. "They call him that 'cause he's always eating."

"How about letting him answer from now on?"

"I was just trying to be helpful."

Dusk was coming faster than I'd expected. The birds had that melancholy sound by then, that nightfall sound.

"We better get there before dark so we can see something," Terhurne said.

"Thanks for the tip."

To Liz he said, "Will you tell this arrogant bastard that all I'm doing is trying to help?"

"I better not. He's mad at me."

"Will you two shut up?"

Liz looked chastened. Terhurne, of course, did not.

"You hear anything about Grieves I haven't?"

"I would've shared it with you if I had, Noah. We had a bargain."

"I didn't know the bargain included you following me. You should've asked if you could go along."

"Would you have let me?"

"Probably."

He snorted. "Now there's a hell of an answer."

But I was wasting time we didn't have. "Let's go."

❖

Flickering ruby light was all that was left when we rode up on a ragged chunk of mountain and gazed down upon the perfect bowl in which the enormous spread of hotel and cabins sat. A half-moon lent the scene a silver patina.

There was a huge dock. Steamboats used to set their wealthy passengers down there. If the visitors were especially important, the staff band would no doubt play for them as they reached the hallowed ground of the resort. There would have been fancy buggies to take them to the three-story hotel with six large cabins angling out from each side. The cabins would have been the exclusive province of the rich and notable. Rich alone wouldn't have been enough. Notable alone might have been enough if it was the right kind of notable.

I wondered where the Turners had gone to. Not only was there no sign of them but no sign of horses anywhere. No lamps or candles in windows, either. Not on our side of the hotel, anyway.

We dismounted. Our animals would go no farther than that. Too easy to spot them.

"There's probably a gun in at least one of those windows," I said. "And one on the other side, too."

"How many men you figure he has?" Terhurne said.

I shrugged. "He wouldn't be stupid enough to try and hide out in there alone. At least a couple, probably three or four."

I took the field glasses and stood on the highest point I could while staying hidden in the trees. The hotel had been designed to give the impression that it was a Scottish castle right out of Sir Walter Scott. And right out of Molly's dreams.

The hotel was a thing of turrets and battlements and towers and gables all seeming to seek heaven in their elegant sweep. Once you traversed the bridge across the moat encircling the castle you reached massive doors that were flanked by huge beasts of Scottish myth. And of course there were windows, large and small, everywhere. In the many wars that had bloodied Scottish soil, the windows had enabled archers to repel enemies down the centuries. A sizable portion of the ground level showed the twisted wood and charred innards where the fire had swept. The fire had taken out nearly half the ground floor but the castle had been built with such care that it remained impervious, it seemed, to structural collapse.

I could picture Molly in one of those windows on a fine spring day waiting sight of her knight on his storied white stallion. Lute music would calm her and dreams of his embrace would soothe her. The king might appear and tell his daughter that she was being foolish. That she was so beautiful and so sought after that of course the knight would come and he would beg for her hand in marriage. And then she would take daughterly solace in the arms of the old king and he would let her sigh and weep however long she wished.

I was looking for any hint of humanity inside. But there was nothing. I wondered if the Turners were still alive. Grieves might have dispatched them quickly once he got their money.

Or maybe it was Grieves who was dead. Maybe for once the Turners were making love to each other instead of strangers before fleeing.

I couldn't see the rear of the hotel from where I

stood. It was likely barricaded in some fashion. Grieves wouldn't have enough men to keep both entrances guarded.

And then I saw it. The middle floor. Burning brilliantly for just a moment. Most likely an oil lamp. And then it passed out of the frame of the window.

The safest way to approach the hotel would be from the back. Two men would be better than one and three better than two. But neither Liz nor Terhurne would be much help. Liz lacked the experience and Terhurne I didn't trust. He might decide to do something on his own that would get both of us killed.

I went back to them. I had a good lie ready and told it well. "I'm just going to get a look at the back of the place. Just to figure out the best way in. If I see a chance I'll take it. And that's when I'll call you both to sweep around back."

"How'll we know?" Terhurne said.

"You ever in the military?"

"Never got a chance."

I figured he had a pretty good lie ready, too. And he told it with fair conviction, the implication being that he'd sure wanted to join but circumstances just wouldn't allow it, those circumstances being, I imagined, that he didn't want to get killed.

I gave them both the whippoorwill whistle we'd used back then. Three distinctive cries repeated three times. I was damned loud.

"I don't think you should go alone. Couldn't we at least go with you to look it over?"

"Liz, three people're a whole lot easier to spot than one."

"I'm pretty good at this sort of thing."

"You may be, Terhurne. But we both agree that one man's got a lot better chance of slipping past them."

Then I made it the way they'd want to hear it: "I sure wouldn't go in there alone. That's why I told you about the whistle. I need you standing by."

Terhurne looked at Liz and frowned. Being left behind with a ninety-pound young woman probably wasn't what he had in mind. He'd leave this part out when he was telling the voters about all the risks he'd taken bringing Grieves in. If he didn't get in my way, I'd probably go along with him. He'd be a dime novel legend in no time.

There was also the chance that he knew I was lying to him. But he wouldn't want to call me on it in front of Liz. I'd embarrassed him enough in front of her.

"You just listen for the whistle."

"I still think you should take us along, Noah."

"I may be whistling before you know it, Liz. I'm sorry but that's the way it has to be for now."

"He's a bullheaded SOB, Liz."

"Look who's talking, Terhurne."

❖

I was back in the war again, behind enemy lines. Night and forests were the best friends I had. The only friends I could trust.

Then as now the idea was to become a shadow indistinguishable from all other shadows so that no matter how wily-eyed the sentry or lookout man, he'd never spot me. Moonsilver had become my favorite color and night birds my favorite music. I'd been forced to learn what was and what was not edible among the plants and undergrowth and thorny bushes. There were several obvious ones that could make you sick or even kill you. Everybody knew those. The ones you had to watch out for were the ones nobody ever talked about.

The closer I got to the resort, the more impressive it looked. I thought of all the murders, the cholera, and the fire that had finally shut it down. There were many myths about the castles of Scotland, including cursed ones. Given the history of the resort, the curse idea would seem to apply. To believers, anyway. I counted myself somewhere in the middle.

There was no bridge over the moat in back. And the massive wooden door had been barricaded with at least twenty two-by-fours. The spacing of the boards was uneven. I imagine it had been boarded up in haste after the fire to keep out looters. Much of the hotel had remained intact and would have been an inviting target to thieves.

The native stone of the castle walls gave the enormous hotel a pleasingly medieval look. Again I had a picture of archers leaning out the windows and killing the attackers below. But then I'd read an awful lot of Sir Walter Scott.

Deep woods provided a semicircle around the hotel. I walked the entire length of them, trying to figure out which would be the best way in. I could swim the moat but I'd leave myself open to anybody who saw me. And even if I tried it, how did I get inside? The double doors leading inside would be closed.

The only possibility I could see was on the west side of the castle where a canoe sat tied to the bank. There was a window on that side of the castle that seemed to be within grabbing distance—if I got very lucky, anyway. There could be a guard inside ready to put a bullet in my forehead as soon as he saw me trying to grapple my way inside. But I didn't see any other way in.

That was when the guard stepped into view in that window. He had field glasses of his own. He scanned the woods.

I stepped back into deeper shadow even though I didn't need to. There was no way he could see me from where he was.

But then he was joined by a second man. They spent a long minute discussing something. The second man took the field glasses and started scanning the woods. He didn't spend much time on the location where I was hiding. Instead he searched for awhile in a place far to my west.

Then the first man took the glasses back and had another look for himself. He, too, spent serious time watching the same area.

They stayed another three or four minutes and then quickly vanished. I wondered what the hell was going on.

What I had to decide was whether that was the time to use the canoe to get to the castle wall and try and hoist myself up with the low window ledge. In the Scotland of a few centuries back, there wouldn't have been windows that far down the wall. Too easy for the attackers to get in. But this was a hotel for rich people and they wouldn't be willing to pay much for a hotel with no windows.

The gunfire started soon after.

I'd been about ready to make my break and run for the canoe but the sound of gunshots caused me to recede even farther into the dark woods.

Shouts. The sound of shots fired back and forth. The great thunderous sound of the front gates parting. Pounding footsteps as the gunfire continued back and forth, back and forth. Somebody would have to reload soon.

Two horses with riders slamming across the bridge over the moat in front. More shouts. In the starshine the horses had the look of paintings, enormous dark animals all bearing around the side of the castle on which I hid. There was no doubt where they were headed. The woods from where the guards' gunfire had been returned.

Meaning that Terhurne and Liz hadn't cared a damn about anything I'd said and had decided to do some skulking on their own. Or that Nan and Glen Turner had been hiding in the woods. But why?

I had to make a decision. With the gates open in front, I could get inside easily. The problem was who might be waiting for me in there. I could easily get killed.

But scrambling up the side of the castle and hoping to hurl myself inside over a window ledge—

Running in through the front gates sounded more promising. I tightened the grip on my Winchester and prepared for a dead run from the woods to the front side of the castle. No sense in moving slowly, checking every few yards to see if anybody spotted me from the castle or the grounds. If I was going to die, I might as well be running.

PART THREE

Chapter 23

I didn't get far before stumbling against a tree and barking my right knee pretty good. But all I could do was keep running.

I had my Winchester. I could fire from some distance and fire accurately. As I worked my way across the open stretch of grass, I heard more gunfire and more shouts from the back side of the castle. I still couldn't decide who it was likelier to be—had Grieves's men found Liz and Terhurne or the Turners? But why would the Turners be fleeing? Presumably, they'd paid Grieves off by then. But then there was the possibility that he wanted both the explosive device, whatever it was, and the money as well.

I thought of the "boom boom boom" sounds Grieves had made, saying they'd make him rich. And what McGivern, the miners' top man, had said about all the noise Grieves had made in the countryside one day. Not to mention what I'd seen at the quarry.

The ground sloped down. I stayed to the long shadows of the few trees that ran east to west ending right at the creek line. I hadn't planned on stopping but then I saw a figure emerge from the front gate and look around.

A sentry, judging from the way he started walking the length of the castle's front, scanning the grounds and the forest beyond as he walked.

Shooting him would be easy. The trouble being that shooting him would also give my position away.

Then more shouting from the rear. The sentry was alert to everything now. He dropped his Winchester into position. He could fire with no problem.

Shouts had now given way to yelling and curses. A male voice. At first I couldn't be sure whose it was but after a brief time Terhurne's boisterous racket came clear.

"You have any idea what you're doing? You're pushing a sworn lawman around. You've already shot at me and that alone could get you ten years in prison."

When they came into view in the moonlight, I saw the two thugs on horses and Liz and Terhurne walking slightly ahead. Both men had their guns trained on them.

Terhurne kept talking. He spoke with lofty authority, reminding the thugs that they had—at least according to Terhurne—just committed one of the most heinous acts in the history of the world.

One of the thugs finally said: "Shut up, old timer, or I'll kill you right here and right now."

"Leave him alone," Liz said. "You're only tough because you've got a gun."

The thug laughed. "You sound like you're pretty tough yourself, young lady."

"Kiss my ass. And stop laughing at me!"

Liz was starting to warm up to the task of insulting these boys into louder and louder laughter. She didn't seem to realize that her words were almost forcing them to laugh.

Terhurne wasn't done yet. "You could let us go right

now and I'd make sure there wouldn't be any charges. I'd be happy to say that you confused us with somebody else and that in the dark it was just a natural mistake, nobody could see what was going on."

The thug responded by shooting Terhurne's hat off his head. Liz scrambled in front of him and picked it up. She presented it almost formally to him, as if she was giving him some important award.

But this time the thug nearest her wasn't so amused. Apparently sick of her holding him up, he kicked her hard in the side. "Now get movin'."

He must have done more damage than it appeared. She grabbed the left side of her ribs and dropped to one knee. She didn't cry but I could hear her whimper even from where I was.

"You touch her again, you'll be sorry."

"Yeah, old man, I'll be sorry, won't I?"

Terhurne wasn't intimidated. He walked over to Liz and helped her up on her feet and took her in his arms. They might have been grandfather and granddaughter. The whimper again. Harder now. I wondered if the bastard had broken a rib.

The thugs slacked off some. They let Terhurne talk to Liz and then let him keep his arm around her as they walked toward the front gate of the castle.

The sentry was still there. He didn't talk to any of them, just nodded. He put his rifle in their general direction.

Their horses sounded heavy and dangerous as they crossed the wooden bridge. Liz and Terhurne vanished from sight beneath the arch of the gate.

The sentry didn't leave his post. He'd most likely stay there for some time, see if he could spot anybody in the forest himself. Grieves was probably nervous. He was in this isolated hotel and within a couple hours of each other the Turners and then Liz and Terhurne show up. He had to be wondering how his hiding place had been discovered all of a sudden.

I needed to get closer. I couldn't count on jumping him from where I was. But as I started to move, the sentry turned and looked in my direction. His rifle barrel came up a bit. Had he spotted me? Cold sweat made me shiver. Now it wasn't just a matter of me getting in there to grab Grieves. It was also a matter of saving Liz and Terhurne.

Never taking his eyes off the area of the tree I was now lurking behind, the sentry started walking my way. Fast. His Winchester was pointed just about where my chest would be.

Chapter 24

He was maybe ten feet from me when he turned abruptly and started stalking toward a large boulder that rested about fifteen yards away. I'd considered that as a hiding place but decided that the tree offered a better position to shoot from if it came to that.

I froze in place. He circled the boulder, his weapon ready. The large rock gleamed like mica in the moonlight. But he wasn't taken with the beauty of it. He just wanted to make sure that nobody was hiding behind it.

He walked around it twice. Maybe he thought that somebody was playing a game of hide-and-seek with him.

When he finished, he walked to the front of the boulder, pushed his hat up with his thumb, and then leaned back against the rock, his Winchester leaning right back with him, and fixed himself a smoke.

He kept scanning the area. He was far enough away that I had managed to become one with the shadows. He spent a long time staring at the tree but then swung his head away, convinced, I guess, that there was nothing worth seeing there.

I could hear voices in the resort, echoing off the

scarred emptiness of the west side of it. Liz screamed and then cursed and then Terhurne cursed and cursed and cursed. There was a single gunshot. My stomach knotted. Had Grieves or one of his thugs killed Liz or Terhurne? They were certainly expendable. They didn't have any money and except perhaps for sex with Liz, they had nothing to trade. And even that, for all her fetching qualities, wasn't much in the way of a trade. If they wanted her they'd simply rape her.

I knew then that I had only one chance to get inside and I had to be ready to take it.

The sentry would pass within ten feet of me—if he took the same way back to the gate. I'd have to jump him there. Ten feet was a problem. I wasn't exactly an athlete. And in midair I'd be vulnerable as hell. All he'd have to do is sense me. And then turn around and start blasting away. That's what I'd do.

I reached down and found a few rocks the size of acorns. They'd have to do.

He stood up, dropped his smoke, killed it with his boot heel. Then he stretched. He was taking his time. He hadn't shown much curiosity about the scream and the lone shot inside the castle. He didn't show a whole lot of curiosity at that point, either. He'd given up looking around. He was either bored or tired or both.

He lifted his Winchester, grabbed it tight, and set off walking slowly back to the castle.

If he didn't respond to my trick in the right way, he'd kill me easy. The thing was to bounce the rocks off the boulder so that he'd turn away from me to see what was making the noise behind him.

That meant I had to move out of the protection of the deepest shadows and stand where he could see me any time he angled his head in the direction of the tree.

I had no choice. I moved slowly. Coyotes and an owl

went to work on the night air. Doing me a great favor. I'd accidentally stepped on a few twigs. The sentry might have picked up the sound otherwise.

I pitched the rocks so that they would land on the top of the boulder, just where it began sloping down to the far side. I just had to hope he would turn left rather than right.

The rocks made more noise than I'd anticipated.

Boredom and fatigue didn't affect him then. He swiveled like a gunny in a dark alley, confronting an enemy he couldn't see.

And the swivel took him in the direction away from me.

My assault wasn't perfect. He saw me just as I'd covered about half the distance between us. He started to raise his rifle. I started to dive through the air for him. I had to land on him before he could get a shot off and alert everybody in the hotel.

I landed hard enough to slam his rifle to his chest. He couldn't squeeze the shot off. I rode him all the way down to the ground, ripping the Winchester from his fingers and already smashing him in the face three or four times before he'd even settled against the grass.

I didn't have much choice but to kill him. He'd be too dangerous to leave alive. I couldn't shoot because of the sound. I could take the bowie he carried and cut his throat but I wasn't much for cutting people. About all that was left was to strangle him and then break his neck so he couldn't come around later. Despite what you may have heard, strangulation is an imprecise method of killing somebody.

I dragged the corpse behind the boulder. The body was busy with its purges. Dying smells.

I had no idea if anybody was watching me from the castle. Not much I could do about it, anyway. I finished hiding the body, grabbed my Winchester, and ran toward the waters of the moat gleaming in the moonlight.

There hadn't been any sounds from inside for minutes. When I got to the bridge, I slowed down. I had to move as quietly as I could. Frogs and crickets and night birds covered some of my entrance.

The first thing I saw was the courtyard, decorated in a style that was supposed to be medieval. There was even a gallery where the king and queen passed judgment on the entertainment that took place in the courtyard. Wide steps led up into the hotel itself.

Except for a few shields and spears and coats-of-arms, the medieval motif was dropped inside the hotel. Then it became, from what I could see in the dark, a very expensive European hotel with vaulted ceiling, small shops, two or maybe even three restaurants, and then the usual concierge's desk, tiny offices for various hotel functionaries, and a check-in desk so long and wide you could probably play tennis on it.

But there was, over it all, the stench unique to a large fire. If anybody ever rebuilt this place, they'd have to deal with the smell. It would be a long time before the odor simply vanished into the air. And it would get only worse as I got closer to the wing that had been burned down.

Silence.

Well, the usual creaks and groans of any large building but nothing else. This was a testament to one of two things. Either none of the people in the building were speaking above a whisper or they knew I was there and were observing me from a place I was unaware of.

Three floors with dozens of rooms. I could spend all night looking for Liz and Terhurne. I thought of the first thing you learned as an agent. It was true in wartime and it was supposedly true at that moment. That nothing mattered but the job you were doing for the government. Anything personal was irrelevant. Meaning, in this case, that my priority should have been Grieves. But I couldn't get Liz from my mind. I didn't like thinking about what they might do to her before they killed her. Most people think that there are no fates worse than death. But they're wrong.

I didn't expect to find much on the ground floor and I was right. I spent fifteen minutes opening office doors onto darkness. All three restaurants had ample window space so spill light from outside made them easy to check. What nights there had been in these places. People from all over the world—rich and powerful people, of course—had spent hours in there. The so-called Frontier West was the selling point. Silks in the evening but in the day you wore costly cowboy clothes purchased in one of the shops I'd just checked out. The clothes were nothing like real range clothes and most of the people looked silly as hell in them but slap them on tame horses for trail rides and they could fancy themselves real true Western folk. Folk who frequently asked, "Is Jesse James anywhere around here?" They'd be photographed endlessly for use later back at home where they'd bore their friends with an interminable reprise of their frontier adventures.

I was just about to try the next floor when my right boot stepped in something slick on the floor to the right of a carpeted stairway.

I hunched down, touched a fingertip to the mess and then gave it a sniff. Blood does have a smell, much as some medical people say otherwise. And there was no doubt this was blood.

The pool of it was at an angle to the central staircase. I tried to reconstruct what might have happened. There had been a single shot. A scream. Somebody had been wounded or killed right at that spot, thus the pool of blood. I then followed the smaller splotches of blood to the staircase itself and could see in the moonlight that the injured or dead person had been taken up to at least the second floor.

The dark at the top of the stairs was rich and deep. Anybody could be watching me from there. I took each of the first steps carefully, slowly, my Winchester aimed right into the center of the gloom above me.

Each tiny noise I made was magnified a hundred times, at least to my ears, in the odd quietness of the place.

On the fourth step I stopped, tensed.

A single sound from upstairs.

The cold sweat came again. This time accompanied by a pounding heartbeat. I was exposed completely there on the staircase.

The sound again. At least this time I had some sense of what was making the sound. A footstep, then another. Easy to imagine somebody getting into position to shoot.

Another footstep. Weight on a wooden floor, a flat spot in that floor, a faint creaking sound.

The first floor was marble. The second was wood.

A bad choice awaited me. Go back or go on? Either way I was a damned good target. I stared hard into the darkness above me. But even though my eyes had adjusted to the worst of the gloom, I still couldn't make out any human shape up there in the shadows.

Then he made it easier for me.

To get the shot he wanted, he had moved away from the side of the staircase to the edge of the top step.

He had a clear shot.

But I fooled him. He was expecting me to stay within the range of his aim. I'd be standing up and running back down the stairs or I'd be hunching down and hugging the side of the staircase.

What I did was throw myself to the far side of the staircase and start rolling back down the steps as quickly as I could.

He fired. He fired four or five times, in fact. His bullets chewed up carpet and they chewed up wood but he wasn't lucky enough to chew me up.

When I rolled back down on the marble floor, I kept right on rolling until I was out of his range, off to the side of the staircase.

A shout from far above me, the third floor: "What the hell's going on down there, Lars?"

"Must be that federal man he told us to watch for."

"You get him?"

"No, but I will."

"You damned well better."

"You the boss now, asshole?"

All this conversation going on in the gloom, no faces attached to it.

I could hear the shooter reloading. He was taking his time. Probably figuring that he was just making me all the more nervous.

What he was making me was mad that I hadn't yet reached the second floor. My only concern was that there might be one or two other men on that floor. It wouldn't be hard to find another way up. But I didn't want to open a door when I got up there and take three bullets in the chest for my trouble.

I took another tour of the first floor. This time I knew what I was looking for. An alternate set of stairs that would take me upward.

The shooter had to know I wasn't dumb enough to try the grand staircase again. He also had to know that I'd be frantically looking for another way to get up there.

It took me longer than I'd expected. Not that there weren't alternate, smaller staircases. There were three others in fact on that vast floor. The problem being that they were all open, exposed. I couldn't get up them without making at least a few small noises. Easy for him to hear me and sit in the darkness, waiting for me.

I even considered the dumbwaiter I found in the kitchen, the problem being that I'd be trapped on it if it made too much noise—trapped and with no easy chance of escaping.

Behind the largest office on the first floor, I found a door that seemed out of place in the sumptuous setting. A plain, unadorned door.

I opened it and found my means of getting to the second floor. Maybe even the third. The management must have used those stairs when they had to get up top quickly. A resort had to have a dozen little emergencies a day.

I started climbing.

The echoes in the narrow stairway were even louder. Not even moving on tiptoe helped all that much. I considered taking my boots off but not knowing what lay on the other side of the door, I decided against it.

The other trouble was the darkness. In effect, I was moving inside a long coffin, sealed without any light getting in at all. I could stumble at any moment. And that would likely be heard by somebody. And the narrowness was getting to me. I've never been one for cramped spaces. We all have fears that can turn us into raving lunatics at the wrong moment. And this was one of mine. It was so tight in there that I could smell myself, sweat, tobacco, gunpowder.

As I went step by step, I kept touching the wall on the right, hoping that its seamlessness would suddenly turn into a door frame. After a few minutes I wondered illogically if I wasn't on a stairway at all but some other passage used for a purpose I couldn't even guess at.

But, finally, the feel of a frame. Then, lowering my hand, the feel of a doorknob. Finally—as long as it wasn't locked.

It turned without any problem at all.

I leaned my sweaty head against the door in a moment of relief. I couldn't get Liz from my mind. I should never have let her come along, the hell with her getting a story that no other newspaper would have.

I set my Winchester against the wall, making sure it wouldn't fall and rattle its way down the steps I still couldn't see. The clatter would be bad enough. What if it also misfired?

I stood up straight, fixed my Colt firmly in hand, and started to ease the door open an inch at a time.

It was when I had gotten the door open just far enough to peek out that the rifle point stabbed at the side of my head and a male voice said, "I was betting you'd find this stairway, Ford, and looks like I was right."

Chapter 25

From what I could see, he was tall, rangy, and looked at least partly Comanche, even though his work shirt and denims weren't what most Indians wore, not even on reservations. He seemed to have a discoloration the size of a silver dollar on the left side of his face, though in the dim light I couldn't be sure.

Also, he wasn't alone. As he took my Colt from me, somebody came up from behind and hit me with enough force to drop me instantly.

I woke up tied to a chair in a small storage room of some kind. Boxes of various kinds were stacked high on all four walls. The Indian and a Mexican sat at a table watching me.

The Mexican reached into the pocket of his vest and extracted a railroad watch. He studied the face of it then handed it across the table for the Indian to see.

"You lose," the Mexican said.

"You bastard. I never win with you." The Indian shoved the watch back across the table. "You didn't bring me any luck, Ford. We bet on how long it would be before you woke up again. I had you at under five minutes. You were out six. Now I have to pay up."

"Glad you two are having such a good time."

"You're lucky we didn't kill you already," the Mexican said.

"Grieves said we should torture you if we don't get what we want."

"I personally enjoy torturing," the Mexican said, "do to you what all them Texas Rangers did to me when I was a young man. But my friend here, he's a Catholic and he says torturing somebody is a mortal sin." He smiled. "Can you believe that, here I'm a Mex and I don't believe none of that Father, Son, and Holy Ghost bullshit, and here he's raised wild and the missionaries get their hands on him and they've got a believer for life."

Though my head hurt, and the trickle of warm blood down my back made me uncomfortable, I couldn't let it pass. I looked right at the Indian. "So torture's a mortal sin but murder isn't?"

"To me it's a worse sin, torture, I mean. You can kill a man clean and leave him die in dignity. But you can't kill a man clean with torture. He has no dignity then. So the torture is a much worse mortal sin."

"Even to a nonbeliever like me, that makes sense. But of course I don't believe in mortal sins of no kind. The priests just tell you that to keep you in line."

I glared at one then the other. "So what is it you two assholes want from me, exactly?"

"You got some mouth, señor."

"At least I don't kill women," I said.

"Who kills women? Not me and the breed here."

"You killed Molly Kincaid."

"Bullshit," the Indian said. "We killed her uncle but we never killed her."

It was simple. I believed him. "Why'd you kill her uncle?"

The Mexican snorted. "Grieves, he was in town one

night all liquored up and he seen this Molly girl and so he gets all crazy about screwing her. But she won't go back to his room so he takes her uncle and her out for some steaks. Figures he'll impress them and get in her that way. But all he does is end up bragging about how he's gonna get rich. But in the morning he can't remember what he told her and her stupid uncle, you see? So he had us kill the old man. He didn't want us to kill the girl because he thought he could still screw her. When it comes to women, man, he don't think logical at all."

"Woman crazy," the Indian said.

"He says he's gonna get into that Turner woman tonight before he kills her and her husband. He'll get the money from them first, though. He ain't that woman crazy."

"And then you kill me."

"You know the kind of people we are," the Mexican said. "This is a lot easier than workin' on a ranch."

I'd always thought that there was a factory somewhere that turned out men like these. They even looked alike no matter what color they were. Rarely shaved, rarely bathed men who preferred grubby clothes and valued only two things—money and the kind of guns they packed. The factory sold them by the dozen. And if you bought two dozen at a time, you got a discount.

"You file any reports on Grieves yet?" the Indian said.

"No."

"What if we don't believe you?" The Mexican this time.

"Then you don't believe me. You asked me a question and I gave you an answer."

"Grieves is afraid you already let Washington know everything. He's real worried you've already sent more federales after him."

"I don't file reports until everything is finished. This isn't finished yet."

The Indian grinned. "You think you'll be around to finish it, do you?"

"I plan to be around. I want to see this grenade for myself."

"How do you know it's a grenade?"

I smiled. "Well, Dobbs's work is in creating handheld weapons. He spent years on different types of grenades. I went out to the quarry and saw what it did to the limestone."

The Indian laughed. "Pretty amazing, isn't it? Think of that on a battlefield. Just think what that grenade can do to people."

I can't tell you when the noises started to build. I'm not sure I heard them at first. But they did go, once I was aware of them, from virtual silence to a tumult of shouts. And then feet slamming down from above—the stairs leading to and from the third floor, somebody descending at a furious pace, shouts behind him then. And then finally gunfire, the thunder of it booming and echoing off the vaulted ceiling and the immense walls.

"Better go see what the hell's going on," the Indian said. "You watch him."

"Thinks he's the boss of me," the Mexican said, his dark eyes unhappy as they watched his partner leave.

More footsteps on the stairs leading down to where we were. Then in quick sequence: the Indian shouting, quick exchange of gunshots, a mortal cry, a body collapsing on the floor.

Another sequence: shouts from those still descending the staircase, more gunfire, somebody rushing toward our room in an abrupt silence.

"Too bad he didn't get killed," the Mexican said presuming, I guess, that it was the Indian scurrying back to our room after the shooting was finished.

He shoved his six-shooter back into his holster. He seemed to be under the impression that whatever had gone wrong—obviously Grieves's men up top had been chasing somebody—that everything was right again.

But that was quickly disproved.

The inward-opening door was flung open and there stood the bloody and ragged figure of Glen Turner. He didn't hesitate, didn't give the Mexican any chance at all. He shot him twice in the face. The Mexican's hand hadn't even had time to drop to his holster. He was blown back against the wall, his skull cracking on impact. He was already long dead.

Turner slammed the door shut, bolted it quickly. "There's only two of them left out there."

He sneered when he saw I was tied to the chair. "The big bad federal man."

"You don't look like you've been doing so well yourself."

"Grieves is a sadist, let me tell you, that boy is ready for the asylum."

"Where's your wife?"

His face, which he valued so much, got ugly. "The way the bitch has treated me lately, I just left her up there."

"You left her with Grieves?"

"Spare me the speeches, Ford. You and I both know what Grieves is going to do to her. The question is do I care and my answer is no. She's slept with everybody else, she might as well sleep with him."

As he said this, he started untying me.

"She slept with you, too. Right, Ford?" Pause, then: "Right?"

Chapter 26

The first thing he did after untying me was to hit me square in the mouth. He might have been something of a fancy lad but in the last few minutes I'd gotten to see that he was good with both gun and fist. I suppose, strictly speaking, that I had it coming, having slept with his wife and all. But I didn't like it and planned to return the favor when I got the chance.

His punch gave me a bloody lip. One punch wouldn't do it for sleeping with his wife, even though he'd apparently cheated on her many times, too. But now wasn't the time to worry about their marriage.

When he moved in for another one, so angry he'd forgotten to cover himself, I sailed a punch of my own in right above his belt. And then as he was doubled over and was staving off vomiting, I rabbit-punched him on the back of his head. He went down to his knees where he hovered for just a moment before he started splashing his last meal all over the place.

He was a good vomiter. Noisy and dramatic. His whole body jerking about the second time a whole bunch of the orangish stuff came up.

Much as I liked being around vomit, I decided to take a look around the immediate darkness outside our room. Before I did that, I grabbed the lantern and turned it out. No sense making myself a target as I was backlit in the doorway.

Behind me, Turner was stumbling to his feet. Quiet he wasn't. He kept bumping into things. I kept looking at the staircase to the third floor and the other staircase down the hall. That would be the right spot to put men in place so that they could sneak up on us. I didn't know how many men Grieves had left. But one or two would be all he'd need to ambush us.

Turner crept out of the door, looking around in the darkness for me. I whispered, "Over here."

When he reached me he said, "We've each got our reasons to get up on that third floor."

He paused, looking around some more. He'd taken the Indian's gun. He now had two of them. "You want Grieves and I want the money and the grenade."

"Not your wife?"

"Hell, he can have her. It's one thing when a man is unfaithful but when a woman is—"

"Spare me. Cheating is cheating."

"That's just minister bullshit." Then, slyly: "You want her for yourself, don't you?"

"No offense but she's a little fast for me."

"Then you're on my side."

I was going to answer his ignorant remark but that was when one or two of them opened up from behind the staircase down the hall.

Two shooters, I knew after counting the bullets in the first assault. We ran for cover behind our own staircase. We returned fire. A muted cry gave me the impression that we'd gotten lucky and that we'd hit one of them.

I could hear the unwounded one talking to him. Not the exact words, the tone more than anything. Trying to convince him he was going to be all right. That they'd get him fixed up real soon. They sure made a lot of noise as they moved around. They didn't have careers as ballerinas ahead of them. If they'd made any more noise they could have shaken the roof. One of them even sneezed.

They could be friends or even brothers from the worried tones of the gunny who hadn't been wounded. He now had two things to worry about. The wounded one dying on him and us trying to kill him.

Now that we were ducking behind the stairwell, it was easier to talk. "I'm going to sneak upstairs and look around. You stay here and hold this one down."

Turner sneered. "Yeah, right. You kill Grieves, get the money and the grenades—and my wife. Holy Matrimony. Or maybe that's a term you're not familiar with."

"Sure, Turner, like you and she practice it all the time. All I want is Grieves and the grenades. Neither Nan or your money interests me at all."

"How'm I supposed to believe that?"

"Right now, I don't give a shit if you believe it or not. Now I'm going to be on those stairs in the full moonlight and our friend down the hall can pick me off with no trouble. As soon as I'm in position to jump onto the stairs and start running, I need you to open fire and keep him pinned down."

"And what if I don't?"

"Then I'll be able to see you from the staircase and I'll kill you on the spot."

❖

By staying to the left side of the staircase, I had a good view of the open area at the top of the stairs. Turner would have a similar view of the right side. If a shooter appeared on either side, one of us should be able to pick him off. That was the theory, anyway.

The problem was keeping relatively calm as I waited for the inevitable battle at the bottom of the stairs to break open. Turner and the other shooter were very much alive and ready to kill each other.

And then I was jarred maybe half a foot off one of the wide marble steps when the gun battle broke out below. Apparently, Turner had put the Winchester I'd left behind to good use.

This wasn't Grieves's "boom boom boom" but within the decorous halls of the hotel, the explosions and echoes of explosions were plenty loud. The gunfire cracked back and forth, back and forth, echoing off the ceiling with enough force to bounce around on the lower floors. The usual curses rang out, too, men agitated by flying bullets, any one of which could kill them.

And then came the cry. And I knew that Turner had made contact. The shooter he'd hit was sobbing, the way you hear young men of all colors, creeds, and courage cry out when they know instinctively that they've been mortally wounded. Even old men sometimes cry out for their mothers for the bullets have reduced them to children again, children reaching out into the dark cosmos for the arms that had held them and the breasts that had fed them.

The shooter cried out in Spanish and I wasn't sure what he was sobbing about; just that he knew he was dying then as his friend had died a little earlier.

All I could do was use that time of gunfire and death to move faster up the stairs, my eyes never leaving the top right of the stairs where another shooter could be hiding. The problem was I couldn't see much of the stairs to my right. And I damned near lost my life because of it. I was five steps from the top when a young gunny raced into view with a carbine. He clipped off two shots that between them took a piece of my shirt at the shoulder and then a piece of flesh from just above my bicep.

But he didn't know how to cover himself. He would've been just fine if he'd wounded me or killed me but a knick on the arm left me just as deadly as ever. I ducked under the unending line of his bullets and got three clean shots off into his chest. And as he started to fall face down on the stairs, I got him in the forehead.

This time, I took the stairs two at a time.

The third floor was still and murky. Windows at either end of the long hall revealed starlight that lent light for a few feet. The center of the hall was in complete darkness. There were probably twenty doors up there. Grieves would be holed up in one of them, in a suite even a sultan would envy.

This was the worst kind of situation. I had no idea where Turner was, so no backup. There were too many doors to open and close without being heard as I moved up and down the hall. And, after counting my bullets, I realized I had eleven shots left.

But at least the real battle was finally at hand. I'd found Grieves. Or was about to, anyway.

I started working the doors, my skeleton key opening them easily. That section of the hotel hadn't been touched by the fire. The first few rooms I searched were as elegant as they'd always been. The view from up there was something only the wealthiest would ever have. You could scan the plains, the forest, the river, and the mountains with godlike sweep. Night had never looked more mysterious or lovely than it did from up there. This was something the astronomers got to see every night but not us mere mortals.

Six rooms and nothing. I kept listening for any kind

of sound as I went in and out of them. Nothing that sounded like a human being moving about.

In the seventh room I found the dead girl. I thought of Grieves's fondness for prostitutes. Given the makeup this one wore, given the gaudy modern dress she'd been wearing, it was easy to forget that she'd been a real human being. Very young, she probably hadn't left the village or hamlet or farm more than a year or two before. Being summoned to that hotel had probably sounded like fun.

The room was strewn with empty champagne bottles and male clothes and underclothes, all belonging to the same man, Grieves no doubt. While waiting for the Turners to show up, he'd had himself a miniature orgy, the thought that he'd become a traitor not seeming to bother him at all.

I took a last look at the girl. Even in the dusky gloom of the room, you could see the strangulation marks on her thin neck. The perfect ending to a perfect orgy. Murder. I was just opening the door, just getting ready to step out into the hall again, when I saw him walking toward me, a sawed-off dangling from his left hand while his right tried the knobs on various doors, making sure they were locked. I couldn't see much of him, he was just a silhouette. Was he just making his usual rounds or had he heard something and was looking to find the person loose up there?

I eased my way back in, closed the door. I could lock it from inside and he'd go right on by. But I needed to take out as many of Grieves's men as I could so that when I finally confronted Grieves I'd have a chance of either killing him or bringing him in, whichever way he wanted to play it.

I left it unlocked and positioned myself so that when

the door opened inward, I'd be hiding behind it. I'd let him get a few feet inside and then jump him.

He never broke stride. Door to door to door at the same pace, always giving the doorknob a good jolt.

Then he got to where I was.

I could hear him curse sharply. The door he hadn't wanted to find. The door that could mean anything. Maybe it had been accidentally left unlocked. Or maybe it held a killer, Ford maybe, the one they were looking for then.

I heard him pull back one of the triggers on the sawed-off. He obviously wasn't a man who liked to take any more chances than he had to. If he had to walk into a situation like that one, he was damned well not going to take any prisoners.

He came slamming in, kicking the door hard and following it by running straight through the door frame and ending up in the center of the room, knocking over a small table for his trouble.

My idea was to hunch down low, throw the door away from me, and fire. But the door didn't move at the rate I expected and by the time it cleared, the thug and I stared at each other in the dim starlight.

"You stupid bastard," Turner whispered. "I could've killed you."

"I doubt it," I said.

I stood up and walked out into the room. "You see Grieves anywhere?"

"I haven't been to the far end of the hall yet."

"I'm pretty sure that's where he's at."

"I just want to get the money back and get the hell out of here."

"And your wife."

He made a face. "And my wife. If you say so. But

you know what? I still think you slept with her, you prick."

"Let's go."

"You're never going to answer me, are you?"

"You hear what I said, Turner? I said 'Let's go.' "

Rolling darkness. A black fog. We pressed on down the hall. Not until we were closer to the end did the darkness begin to fade somewhat because of the light through the hall window.

A sob.

I froze like a dog on point. Apparently Turner hadn't heard it. He kept walking. Finally realizing that I wasn't two steps in back of him any longer, he turned and saw me.

I put my finger to my lips to quiet him. I touched my ear. Faintly but definitely, the sob again.

He nodded to the door on my left. I nodded. I put up a halting hand and then made my way to the door. Pressed my ear to it.

The sobbing was persistent. Sometimes piercing, sometimes muffled. I waved Turner over. "Cover me."

He nodded. Raised the sawed-off.

I put my hand on the knob, half-expecting it to be locked. And I was right. I dug in my back pocket for my assorted burglary tools. Got the correct one. Went to work.

I nodded to Turner.

The doorknob yielded to the right and I flung the door inward, at just about the same moment diving across the threshold and landing on carpet. A pretty dramatic leap and a textbook example of how you enter a room packed with potential enemies.

That is, a textbook example if the room happens to contain enemies.

Liz and Terhurne were what it happened to contain.

They were lashed back to back, set in the middle of the floor.

The noise I'd heard was Liz cursing and trying to be heard through the gag that had been put in her mouth.

Terhurne was less upset. He just watched us as we walked over to him.

"I almost don't feel like setting you two free," I whispered to them. "I told you to wait for my signal so you go ahead and get captured and tip Grieves off that I was coming."

Liz had plenty to say about that. Really angry. Fortunately for me I couldn't understand any of it. She was still gagged.

"Do you know who he is?" she said quietly after I took off the gag. She was glaring at Turner.

"Yeah. Right now he's helping us."

"He and his wife are traitors."

"We'll get to that later."

"Sanctimonious little bitch," Turner muttered, defending his honor.

"What did he say?"

"Nothing. Calm down, Liz." Then: "You know where Grieves is?"

Terhurne, trying to struggle to his feet, and showing his age in the process said, "Next to the end of the hall on the west side is a double suite. He's holed up in there. There's a boat coming for him tomorrow morning down at the dock there."

"Who else is in there?"

Terhurne nodded to Turner. "Your wife, for one. And two bodyguards."

"We can handle two of them," Turner said.

"You're forgetting something," Terhurne said. "He's got twelve hand grenades in there with him."

"They were supposed to be *my* hand grenades," Turner said.

"Aren't you interested in how your wife is?" Terhurne asked.

Turner looked exasperated. "She's probably having sex with him."

Terhurne's eyes lowered. "He pretty much raped her."

"Pretty much," Turner mocked.

"She didn't give in until he hit her so hard she was unconscious," Liz said. Then: "You're some kind of man. You sell out your country and then you won't even stick up for your wife."

Turner smiled, "What a sanctified lot of people you all are. Want to sing some hymns before we break in on Grieves?"

"I need a gun," Terhurne said. "Mine's in Grieves's suite."

"Ford and I can handle this," Turner said.

"The hell with that," Terhurne said. "I want a gun."

"Look, Terhurne. Turner's right. We're better off with just two of us getting into that suite. Too much chaos otherwise.

"You'll never get in there," Terhurne said. "They'll kill you the second they hear you at the door."

"We're not going to use the door," I said.

"You going to fly in, are ya?" Terhurne said.

"No," I said. "If I remember right from when I scouted the place, that side of the building has balconies."

Chapter 27

A short steel maintenance ladder bolted to the side of the third floor exterior and accessed through a window took us easily enough to the tiled roof. I scrambled up it and Turner followed. The slant of the roof was deep. I had to move carefully. Even though it was tiled, it didn't allow for any serious mistakes. You could slide right off and drop three floors down. If you were lucky, you'd hit the moat. If you were unlucky, you'd be laid up for a long time. Or if your neck turned just the wrong way on impact, you might even go right up to heaven with all your other friends.

And getting on the roof was the easy part.

Even though Grieves might not be expecting us to drop down on his balcony, his thugs wouldn't have any problem opening fire on us. We'd actually be more vulnerable standing on the other side of glass than we would standing on the other side of an oak door.

The only hope we had was surprising them. They'd be expecting us but that didn't mean they'd be in the room that opened on the balcony. If we could get into that room before they did, we'd increase our chances of shooting them first.

Lying flat on the edge of the roof I slowly lowered

my head to see into the room off the balcony. No light. Voices in another part of the double suite.

At any time someone could walk into the room. We needed to move quickly.

For the first time, Turner acted afraid. "These heights are getting to me."

"Not a hell of a lot we can do about that. Hurry up."

"You slept with her, didn't you?"

A man obsessed.

"What the hell do you care? You don't care if she lives or dies."

"Yeah, but if you slept with her, that means I still owe her one."

All he could think about was avenging his honor, if that's what it was. Not exactly the kind of man you wanted in a dangerous situation.

If we both got out of this alive, it was going to be my pleasure to slap Turner around for a couple hours.

He finally shut up and took his position lying flat on the roof, ready to slide off to the balcony below.

I peered over the edge again. The room off the balcony was still dark.

I went first, dropping head first to the balcony floor. A large window displayed the interior of the room; a door next to it led inside.

My landing had been relatively quiet. Turner landed like a heavy iron safe dropped from some distance.

We waited in nervous silence to see if anybody had heard him.

The dark room remained dark.

The door wasn't locked. We filed in quietly.

Voices came from our right. I needed a minute to adjust to the darkness, to see where the pitfalls lay in terms of various furnishings to bump into or stumble over.

This room was a formal dining room. I could make out a long table, eight chairs, candle holders. I wondered how they kept it warm in bitter winter, so close to the balcony and all.

We wasted no time, found the hall that led to the voices.

I knew damned well there was only one way in and that was straight in. Stamp the door in and run in behind a burst of gunfire. Preferably, I'd get Grieves out of there alive. He might be useful to Washington. As would—though he didn't seem to realize it yet—Turner.

But at that moment all that mattered was getting in the room.

"Why the hell haven't they come back yet?" a harsh male voice said.

"Look, Mr. Grieves, they know what they're doin'. This is a big hotel."

"All that gunfire, they should have been back by now," Grieves snapped. "And don't tell me otherwise."

"Just because there was gunfire doesn't mean anything. They had a shootout with Ford. Maybe Ford got away and they're lookin' for him, is all it means." This was a third male voice.

"What the hell's going on here? I lost half my men tonight." Grieves again.

"You're forgettin' what else you got, Mr. Grieves," one of his men said. "You got them grenades."

We were too close to the door to allow for even a whisper. I pointed to it and nodded my head. I was ready to move.

Turner nodded back.

Deep breath. Gripped my gun even harder. Raised my foot.

And then damned near put my foot and half my calf through that door. Shouts, curses, scrambling noises all erupted before the door even started to fling backward. The gunfire was instant on both sides. We'd had the benefit of surprise. They wanted to even things up with a barrage of bullets.

By the time I was across the threshold, I'd taken out the one just inside the door. By the time Turner got across the threshold, the one over by the window was down, too.

But something had happened. I'd only gotten a glimpse of Grieves as he was virtually diving through the door that opened on the hotel corridor.

A cry went up from Turner, distracting me from Grieves momentarily.

I only needed a quick glance to see why he had cried out. The nude body of his wife, her throat slashed, lay next to a couch, as if simply dropped there and forgotten.

I could hear Grieves running down the corridor. He was firing a gun for no special reason. I wasn't chasing him as yet. Maybe the sound of the gunfire reassured him that he was going to get away after all.

Turner was useless now. And I was glad to see it. Whatever love he'd once felt for his wife had returned in this terrible moment and he knelt next to her, holding her hand as if he was once more her true and faithful husband.

I went after Grieves.

By then, he had a pretty good lead. But he was still in sight as he neared the staircase leading downstairs.

He fired on an empty cylinder and tossed the gun away. He jerked another Colt from his belt and got off one more shot before disappearing down the staircase.

He was on the bottom step just as I reached the top one. He turned right and vanished.

I took the steps two at a time.

He'd run into something in the darkness. I heard a heavy object scrape across a piece of uncarpeted floor. And then I heard him curse the way you do when you've accidentally hurt yourself.

He fired off another angry shot. He was reassuring himself again, I guess. I was nowhere within range. In fact, I couldn't even see him.

Then I turned the corner and confronted a small nook filled with overstuffed chairs. One of them stood at an angle in the pathway. This was apparently what he'd run into in the darkness.

He damned near killed me.

The bullet came so close to my left ear that I felt the heat of it sear past me.

He was hiding behind a heavy couch down at the opposite end of this nook where people came to read magazines and gaze outside at the dock. When a steamboat or a schooner came in, I imagined it was quite an elegant sight.

Then it happened. Grieves saw him way before I did. Terhurne had heard all the noise of the chase and gunfire. He had also managed to find a firearm somewhere. He'd followed the gun battle by ear and then come to join me.

But he hadn't been careful.

He got about six feet from me, in a crouch but not enough of one, and Grieves picked him off clean.

Two shots.

As I started to turn around, the top of his head came off in a chunk of white hair and blood.

Liz screamed. She was back there at the bottom of the stairs.

"Stay back!" I shouted.

Grieves must have thought I was distracted because

he started pumping shots my way. Liz was out of range as long as she stayed where she was. None of his shots did much but rip up the top of the squat chair I was crouched behind.

There were two more exchanges of gunfire. Neither of us scored.

I finally said: "You're going back to D.C., Grieves, and you know it. Why don't you go back on your feet?"

His response was another bullet.

I responded in kind, of course, and that was when I heard it. It's a very distinct sound and I've never heard it mimicked with any success. It doesn't necessarily mean death but it certainly means serious injury.

And it's rarely loud. It's just this sound of pain as a bullet sinks deep into flesh or smashes bone. A ragged intake of breath and something like a moan.

I'd hit him and maybe bad.

❖

Waiting.

Trying to figure out if he was wounded or dead or just faking it to make me do something stupid, like stand up.

No sound at all from down there.

I started calculating my chances of moving through the nook itself, crawling my way between the pieces of furniture until I was within a few yards of him.

He'd hear me coming. No doubt about that. And there would be times when I'd be in the open, between furnishings.

But it still seemed less of a chance than trying to reach him in the open path between us then.

I started moving. Every inch I crawled seemed to resonate off every wall.

By the time I'd gone several feet, working myself behind a long couch and then scurrying quickly to reach a chair three feet away, I expected him to start firing.

Maybe he really was wounded badly. Or dead.

I got closer by maybe another ten feet when I heard him shift position. My movements were loud in quarters that close but so were his.

The heaviness of the movement convinced me that I'd hit him. He was dragging himself across the floor. I wasn't sure where he was planning to go but wherever it was, he wasn't going to get there easily.

I pumped two shots at him. Unhinge him a little. Make him know that I was ready to hit him again the first time he gave me any opportunity at all.

The heavy dragging again. I crawled closer. He almost hit me again, the bullet shattering a vase on a table less than a foot from my head.

But given the sound that came after that, I realized he'd fired more as a diversion than to try and kill me.

It took me a few seconds to recognize the sound.

Stairs behind him. Going down them carefully. The wound probably making him cautious. Falling down stairs would be the end of him. I could get to him with no problem.

I jerked myself to my feet and took the chance of charging his position behind the chair.

From there I was able to see two things—the short flight of stairs leading to the casino and the heavy blood trailing behind him like a dark wiggling snake shining in the moonlight.

I had to be more careful as I approached the top of the stairs. He wasn't making any sound then. He could pick me off with no trouble if I just popped up like a target on the top step.

I stopped a few feet short of the step. Listened again. Then—the dragging sound. A heavy door being opened.

I jumped to the third step and started jumping every other one.

Just as I reached the door at the bottom of the stairs, he put three bullets through the wood, forcing me to throw myself back against the wall. Any one of them could have killed me.

I waited until I heard him moving on the other side of the door. I also heard something else this time—him slumping against something, most likely a wall.

The blood was even thicker down there than it had been upstairs.

This time, it was my turn to put a couple of slugs through the door, after which I slammed through it, hitting the floor as soon as I crossed the threshold.

He was crouched down in the entranceway to the casino. The walls around the doors were covered with designs of dice, poker cards and chips, and a squirrel cage.

In the moonlight I could see that he was holding something in his hand.

He was only too eager to tell me what it was. "You've never seen a grenade like this one, Ford."

"Don't be stupid, Grieves. You need a doctor."

"Oh, sure, I need a doctor. Then he'll fix me all up so you can take me back to Washington."

"You made your choice, Grieves. You didn't give a damn about selling out your country."

He laughed. It sounded pained. "Hell, you're no more of a patriot than I am. You went through the war. It's all bullshit. All governments are bullshit."

"Maybe some are less bullshit than others. Now put the grenade down before I shoot you."

The pained laugh. "Won't work, my friend. You have to reload and I know it. And by the time you even start, I'm sailing this right over to you."

He'd counted bullets, a trick you learn from the agency. In mellerdramas, shootouts go on forever without anybody reloading. Real life is a little different.

What he hadn't counted was the Colt I'd taken from one of the dead men in Grieves's own suite.

I dropped my Colt into my holster. And then I reached behind my back and took out the other Colt.

I showed him the gun.

"Maybe there aren't any bullets in that one, either."

He had started to wheeze. Blood was in his throat.

"You wouldn't have time to stop me, anyway," he said. And then he pulled the pin.

From the door behind me, Liz shouted, "Noah!"

I killed him just as he started to hurl the grenade. Two quick bullets through his forehead.

His head slumped to his chest. The hand with the grenade opened and—

I started running back toward the door, Liz shouting all the time.

I didn't make it, of course. The explosion came just as I saw Liz hold the door open. But I still had a long way to go.

In the fury of flame and smoke, I felt the floor begin to sway beneath me. In an instant I remembered things people had told me about being in earthquakes. How the very ground beneath you gave way.

And it was giving way them as the floor between the casino and me started to rip apart and the ceiling down by the casino start to rip and crumble and crash.

All this in a few seconds.

And then the concussion of the explosion itself did me the favor of hurling me through the door Liz was holding open . . .

We huddled on the stairs leading to the casino as the destruction continued. Powerful as the explosion had been, its major impact was confined to the area of the casino. The structure had been built so well it was able to limit the breadth of damage.

But no amount of sound architectural planning could do much about fire. There would be no limiting this damage.

Liz helped me to my feet, trying to get a look at a long gash on the side of my head. But there wasn't time for that.

We made our way up the short stairs to find another way out of the building before the flames took it entirely. Unlike the previous fire, this one wasn't going to leave anything intact.

By the time we found a back stairway and had reached the moat, the fire was on the third floor. I was pretty sure that the rest of the grenades were somewhere in the double suite Grieves had occupied. We needed to be even farther away before the fire reached them.

We dove into the chilly water of the moat and swam to the other side. I dragged myself up to the grass and then reached down and pulled Liz up.

We started running for the forest. She stumbled twice and I half-dragged her after that.

We hadn't quite reached the woods when the fire found the extra grenades. We ran to the cover of the forest and then watched the explosion. Or explosions, plural.

Each one ripped away part of the castle façade. And each one lowered the height of the castle, too. It was exploding and imploding, part of a turret being flung afire into the night, the castle sinking even more.

It was too big a structure to be completely demolished but over the course of the next half hour it was broken and seared into chunks and sections of smoldering ruin.

Liz decided to tear off a piece of my wet shirt and treat the abrasion on the side of my head.

"You could always tear your own shirt," I said.

"Yes, but that just might give you ideas."

"The way you tell it, I'm too old to have ideas."

"Yeah, but you just might surprise me and then what would I do?"

Chapter 28

Knut wanted to have a meeting with the mayor and the rest of the town council so that I could explain what had happened. I also told him to ask Will McGivern, the man who represented the miners.

Knut set the meeting up at the Rotary dining room for that night. It was a long, narrow place with a wine-colored rug and a lighter red shade for the walls. The three paintings were imposing enough, three stout and true men of the West, each of whom had his right hand on his right lapel just the way the painter had told him to. They probably would have been more impressive if I'd had any idea who they were.

I sat next to McGivern. On the other side of me was Liz.

"I know it was you got me invited here. Thanks."

"My pleasure."

Just before I was to stand up and discuss everything that had happened—I owed it to the town after Grieves gave the agency such a bad name—Ella Coltrane and Swarthout came in.

They both looked angry. Swarthout said, "I'm not happy, Knut. We should have been invited."

I said, "I told them not to invite you."

"You've got nerve, if nothing else," Ella Coltrane said.

"If you're going to stay, sit down and shut up," I said to her.

They both looked as if they wanted to express their great indignity at being treated this way but then they decided to just sit down instead.

"Well," Knut said, "I'm going to turn things over to Mr. Ford here. He'll explain everything. And after we've all discussed it and asked him our questions, they'll be serving the food. It's excellent here. Porterhouse steak and mashed potatoes and fresh vegetables and apple pie."

I'd planned on cutting my explanation short, anyway, but the mention of porterhouse steak and apple pie made me keep my little speech even shorter than I'd planned.

Amazing what you can accomplish in eight minutes if you really put your mind to it. When I was finished, I smiled in the direction of Ella and Swarthout. "There were a few other people who tried to get the grenades and sell them so they could make up for certain business losses—you know, like a mine tapping out—but they didn't have much luck."

Swarthout pounded the table with his fist. "You'll regret those words."

"No, I won't, Swarthout."

One of the council members said, "With the sheriff dead, who'll be taking his place?"

Another council member said, "Why, Knut, of course. Isn't that right?"

Knut blushed. I didn't blame him. Sometimes praise is even more embarrassing than insult.

He stood up when they started applauding. "This is all because of Noah Ford here. We'd all gotten the impression that all federal men were as bad as Grieves. But Noah taught us better."

Now it was my turn to blush.

And my turn to stand. I gave them ten seconds of applause then waved them off. "There's one thing I'd like to finish with." I nodded to McGivern sitting next to me. "There's a reward for helping bring Grieves in. We sure wouldn't have wanted the grenades in enemy hands. And I wouldn't have known what we were looking for if McGivern here hadn't given me the information about the explosions Grieves was causing out in the woods." I knew what I was saying was a bit of fact-twisting—I certainly would have come to the same conclusion without McGivern pointing me in that direction—but given the state of the mines and the miners, I wanted to help them in some way.

"The reward is $10,000 and I'm asking Washington to give it to McGivern here to set up a fund so that the miners can feed their families while they're looking for a silver strike of their own."

Swarthout and Ella both looked suitably pissed off, which was enjoyable to see. They'd be pushing on, now that they were broke, to find other silver strikes—if somebody would loan them the money.

"So let's hear some of that applause for McGivern here," I said.

The meeting broke up then. The entire town council took turns shaking McGivern's hand. They were all on the same side now. The town needed a silver strike to survive.

Liz had taken notes throughout the meeting. When she finally put her pencil down, she said, "You know something, Noah?"

"What?" I said, expecting that she'd decided I would be a suitable lover after all.

"If you were even six or seven years younger, I think I'd sleep with you."

"Well, gosh, thanks."

"But I'll tell you what I will do. I'm going to make you a supper tomorrow night you'll never forget."

I laughed. "You may have to handcuff me to keep me in line."

"A man your age'll probably be asleep halfway through the meal, anyway."

Then she poked me in the side. "There's always the chance you could get me drunk and I'd forget my principles."

Chapter 29

I enjoyed the cold air. I sat on the edge of the wooden sidewalk and rolled myself a cigarette and watched the last of the stragglers empty the saloons. The only ones who'd hang on till closing time were the drifters and the town drunks. The stragglers were working men. And dawn came early.

I was thinking back through everything I'd learned that night.

Longsworth came up with his formidable briefcase. "Hear the meeting went well."

"Well as could be expected." He set his briefcase between us, sat down, and got his pipe to going. "Tomorrow morning I'm buying myself a train ticket. Friend of mine from law school says there's a slot open in his office in Cheyenne. I've got to go now or it'll be gone soon. Pretty nice office. Prestigious."

"I thought you were against prestigious. Figured you for a lone gun."

"Yeah," he said, "and look where it got me. I want to settle down with a wife and kids. I'm older than I look. I've got to do it now."

We sat there, Longsworth starting to shiver, smoking and watching the last of the wagon traffic drag by.

"Too bad about Terhurne."

"Too bad about everybody," I said.

"I'm still sorry I didn't get to know Molly. She could've had just about any man she wanted in this town. And she wasn't here that long."

That made me wonder about something. "How long were they in town before I got here?"

He thought back. "Three weeks, I guess. But everywhere Molly went, you could see men lined up behind her. Knut arrested the old man a day after they got here. The old man was doing some fancy stuff with poker over at one of the saloons. Molly had to plead with him not to put her uncle in jail." He laughed. "A gal who looked like that, she'd be pretty hard to turn down. And you know Knut and women."

"No, I guess I don't."

"Everybody around Terhurne liked women just fine."

"So they were here three weeks, huh?"

"Yep. Just enough time for the old man to try every grifter's trick in the book." Then: "Too bad Hayden was over at the café flirting with that new gal. And too bad Knut was over at the livery tryin' to find out why his horse was limping."

He said it. It happens that way sometimes. He said it and it went past me. I'm not a wizard. It went right past me.

"Yeah," I said, "too bad."

He stood up. "Well, I got to get back and finish my packing." He put out his hand and we shook.

A decent young man. I wished him luck.

He picked up his briefcase. "Night."

"Night," I said.

I slept well. No bad dreams. Not even waking up to piss. In the morning, I went over to the café and ate a breakfast that could have handily fed two. Then I walked over to the livery to see how much I could get for my horse and saddle. We settled on a reasonable price. I spent a good long while with the animal so my goodbye was sloppy and melancholy. He'd done much better by me than a lot of humans had.

At the train depot I bought a one-way ticket to St. Louis for the following day. I didn't want to miss Liz's meal later that evening so I had to stay the extra day.

There was a new man behind the front desk at the sheriff's office. He was middle-aged, running to fat, but in his khakis and his Colt, he looked serious and competent.

"Morning," he said. "Help you with something?"

"Knut around?"

"Over to the courthouse. Should be back in a while."

He'd been sitting on the edge of the desk going through a stack of official-looking pages. "You're the federal man, right?"

"Right."

He nodded. He put out a hard slab of hand and we shook. "Name's Dave Evans."

"Glad to meet you, Dave. Wondered if I could take a look at one of the cells back there. The one Molly Kincaid was in."

"Sure."

I carried a cup of coffee back to the cell. Dave walked with me. No idea what I was looking for. And a good thing, too, because I didn't find anything.

Though a lot of people dispute this, sometimes just sitting in the place where murder happened can give you certain ideas—insights, I suppose—that you couldn't get anywhere else. I suppose that's what I was hoping to get back there at that point.

The door opened up front and a woman, sounding troubled, said, "Knut, Knut, where are you?"

Dave sighed. "That's Emma, Knut's wife. She don't trust him much. She stops in here three or four times a day looking for him. Someday he's gonna learn how to treat her. Or he better. She'll leave him if he don't."

He went up front while I stayed in the cell a few more minutes. But nothing about Molly's murder came to mind.

I walked up front to where Emma stood and suddenly, for no good reason at all, a number of things connected in my mind.

Knut had lied to me about being home in bed while Molly was being killed. Longsworth had told me that Knut had been at the livery. Which meant he wasn't far from the jail during the time Hayden was at the café. And then I remembered the scene with his wife Emma in the alley that morning. Her rage and tears. I hadn't known till the moment when Emma came into the sheriff's office that Knut ran around on her. And he'd known Molly since she first came to town—he'd arrested Uncle Bob for cheating at cards. So he'd known her . . . Known her maybe a lot better than most people realized. But maybe Emma realized it . . .

But the lie was what did it more than anything. He could've stopped in at the sheriff's office at any time during the period Molly was alone in there . . .

Emma's pretty face was fixed with anger. At that moment you couldn't imagine that this slight, attractive woman had ever smiled or laughed in her life. Quite the opposite, really. She could easily be one of those women you read about who shot or stabbed her husband. She just went crazy one day and couldn't take whatever kind of trouble her husband was always putting on her.

"Morning, Emma."

She turned away from me so I couldn't see her face. She didn't acknowledge me in any way. I was interrupting a private conversation she was having with the deputy. She was embarrassed.

I walked straight on out the door, embarrassed for her. I got outside and went over to the general store and got myself a sarsaparilla and sat on the bench in front of the store and started to make my plans.

I'd pretty much convinced myself that Knut had murdered Molly. What I had to figure out was how to confront him with it. There wasn't any hard proof. But there were plenty of reasons to suspect him.

Chapter 30

I was standing on the courthouse sidewalk when I saw Emma pull up in the buggy. She just sat there. She would look at me and then look at the double doors of the courthouse.

The day was warming up. The shopping ladies looked pretty as spring flowers as they passed by on their way to the various stores. From where I stood I could see the depot and all the people waiting to board the train that was getting ready to depart.

Knut came out alone. He wore a dark business suit and a white Stetson. He carried some rolled-up papers in his hand. He saw Emma before he saw me. He waved to her. She didn't wave back. I remembered how angry she'd been in the sheriff's office. She was still that mad, apparently.

When he saw me, he smiled. "I thought you'd be long gone by now, Noah."

"Not yet. Got one more piece of business to wrap up."

"Well, good luck with it." He nodded the Stetson toward the street and Emma. "The wife's waitin' on me. We've got some bankin' business we have to do. So I better be movin' along. You wouldn't know it to look at her but she's got a temper."

He started to walk past me. I grabbed his arm.

He looked startled, confused. "Hey, Noah, what the hell's this about?"

"You killed Molly."

"What the hell are you talking about?"

I laid it out for him quickly.

"And that's why you think I killed Molly?"

"I'm going to ask the governor to send his own investigator down here. Ten to one he finds out you had an affair with Molly."

He glanced at the street. As did I. The buggy was empty.

His hand dropped to his holster. "You know I could always arrest you."

"Yeah, you could. But then you'd be in a lot of trouble with the federal boys. And that still wouldn't change the fact that you killed Molly."

I recognized the poke immediately. Cold steel. She had come up behind me. She stood only inches away so nobody could see the gun barrel she'd shoved into my back.

"Emma—" Knut started to say. "Maybe this'll only make things worse."

"We're going in the buggy. The three of us. And we're going to take Ford for a ride in the country."

Knut looked confused. He knew what she was hinting at as well as I did. A nice ride in the country to find a nice deep burial site.

He leaned in then and ripped my Colt from my holster. He jammed it down the front of his trousers. "I guess this is the only thing we can do."

At that particular point the sidewalks were clear and there weren't any more people coming out of the courthouse doors. Emma nudged me with her gun and started me walking straight ahead to the buggy. I assumed I'd have my one and only chance at the time I was stepping up into the buggy. I didn't know how I would handle it yet. I'd have to see how it played out.

When we reached the buggy, Emma left and walked around the far side of the vehicle. She got up in the seat and sat there with her gun held low so passersby couldn't see it. She aimed right at my chest. I should have been nervous but what I was, was curious. She wore a yellow blouse with a black cotton vest over it. The vest was decorated with seven small silver studs on each side. Except one of the tiny studs was missing. The same kind of stud I'd found in the cell where Molly had been murdered.

They were smart people. Knut took her place behind me. "I don't want to shoot you, Noah. You just get up there and sit down." He held the gun up against the back of my head for a moment then nudged me to the wagon.

The break I'd hoped for just wasn't there. Not with two guns on me. No matter what I did, one of them was sure to kill me. I didn't have any idea how they'd explain killing me to anybody. I doubted they did, either. But right then they weren't worried about afterward. They were only worried about getting me out of town.

In a different situation, the three of us sitting in the same seat would have been funny. It was a small buggy, comfortable for two, or three if the third was a child. I was a little bigger than most children. So we were all squirming, elbowing each other, sighing, cursing, as we left town.

I was hoping that the sight of us all packed in this way would alert a citizen or two that something was wrong. We got a lot of waves. A lot of "Howdy's" and a lot of quick interested stares but nobody seemed to see anything odd about us being packed in that way.

We didn't talk. There didn't seem to be much to say. Emma knew Knut had killed Molly and I knew Knut had killed Molly and Knut knew Knut had killed Molly. We were beyond Knut pleading to be let go. He knew I wouldn't let that happen. Leaving him with only one option, finding a good spot to start shoveling.

Knut said, "I'm sorry about this."

We had just reached the town limits sign. The day was starting to get pretty warm. Spring flowers were cast across the prairie and all the way up into the foothills ahead of us. A fawn stood in the underbrush, watching us.

"If you were sorry, Knut, you wouldn't go through with this."

"He wouldn't have chased women, either," Emma said. "You don't know what it was like for me. Every time I'd walk down the street and see a pretty woman, I'd have to wonder if she'd slept with my husband. That's the sort of thing that can make you crazy."

She cracked the reins. The horse broke into a trot.

"Was she going to blackmail you, Knut? That why you killed her?"

He seemed confused, not sure what to say. Then, in a soft voice: "No, she wasn't trying to blackmail me."

"Then I don't understand why you'd kill her."

He stared off across the prairie.

"None of this would've happened if he'd been true to me," Emma said. Her rage was a terrible burden. I knew the feeling. Hating somebody so much that you can't get them out of your mind. You can only think of vengeance. And you think of it just about every minute you're awake. But she was doubly damned. She was in love with the man she hated. And that was the worst burden of all.

The site we found was off a trail that wound through dense forest. Loamy soil made digging relatively easy. The river glistened down at the bottom of the hill shining through branches like sparkling diamonds. The forest smelled clean and good with spring.

Knut did the digging. Emma sat on one small boulder and I sat on another. She kept her gun on me the whole time.

Emma couldn't let go of it. "You couldn't keep your word, could you, Knut? You know how many times you promised you'd give it up? I don't. I lost count by the third year of our marriage. But you'd never last long, would you? Two, three weeks would go by and then you'd start coming home late. You must've thought I was pretty dumb, that I wouldn't know what was going on."

Knut just kept digging. He wouldn't look at either of us.

To me, Emma said, "A couple of them fell in love with him. And one of them was married. I almost told her husband. Can you imagine that? I go up to one of the most important men in town and tell him that my husband and his wife are sleeping together?" She snorted a laugh. I hadn't realized until then that there was a good chance she was insane. I felt sorry for her. Living the way she had, heartbreak after heartbreak and loving him too much to leave—most people would be insane.

"I'm glad we never had no children. You couldn't bring them up in a household like we had. Their daddy traipsing in at all hours, just reeking of the whores he'd laid down with. I'd wash his long johns and I'd see the stain in the crotch from how he'd finished up with her. And sometimes I couldn't even pick 'em up. I'd just leave 'em there for days and days and he'd have to wear the same long johns over and over again." This time there were tears in the corners of her eyes. "You couldn't raise a kid in a household like that."

When Knut got done, he speared the shovel into the ground and said, "I guess we're ready." He seemed embarrassed, tried to look at me, couldn't. A tall pile of dirt lay on one side of the grave.

I readied myself. I had judged that the run between the boulder I sat on and the path was approximately twenty feet. If I rolled over suddenly across the boulder and rolled another four or five feet then stood up and ran—I wasn't just going to stand up and let them kill me. This was one of those times when getting shot in the back was a medal of honor. At least I'd tried to escape.

"This won't be easy for me, Noah," he said. "I mean, if that makes any difference." Then, "You rather sit or stand?"

And then I did it. Simple enough if I was twenty. Not so simple then when I was forty.

I rolled myself over backward on the top of the surface and then started rolling toward the woods.

He started firing immediately. I was too easy a target on the ground. So I jumped to my feet and started running zigzag to avoid the bullets blazing through the air. None of them striking me.

That was when I stumbled. Point of my boot stuck in a small hole. Enough to drop me to one knee. Enough to give Emma time to run after me. I'd just gotten back on my feet when she started firing.

I reacted without thinking. I fired back, shooting her in the shoulder and then the thigh. I stepped over to her and picked up her gun.

During the ten seconds it had taken me to fire, Knut could have killed me easily. But he hadn't. And now as I turned to face him, I thought about all the bullets he'd blasted at me right after I'd started rolling on the ground. None of those bullets had hit me, either.

I faced him now. We were pointing guns at each other.

Emma was sobbing. I didn't intend to look over my shoulder to see how she was doing.

"One of us is going to be dead real soon," I said to him. "And it's probably going to be you, Knut. Why didn't you kill me when you had the chance?"

"Tell him the truth, Knut."

"You shut up, Emma, or I'll come over there and shut you up!" His anger was ugly. There was something he really didn't want her to say.

"Put your gun down, Knut, or I'll have to kill you. I'm tired of this whole thing and right now killing somebody would suit me just fine."

He said, "I've never killed anybody, Noah. I'm not sure I can."

"You're a deputy."

Between sobs, Emma shouted, "He's real high-minded about not killing people. But it don't bother him to cheat on his wife."

When he dropped his gun, she shouted, "Tell him, Knut, or I will."

And that was when he put his hands to his face and started crying. His shoulders shook with his tears. "This is all my fault, Noah. All my own stinking fault."

And then I knew what was going on there. I turned to Emma. The shoulder was bleeding pretty badly.

"You killed Molly, didn't you, Emma?" The jealousy, the silver stud that had fallen off her vest, the fact that Knut tried so desperately to take the blame—

"I'm so sorry, Emma," Knut said. "I'm so damned sorry for all I've done to you."

I looked back at Knut. I felt almost as sad as he did.

They wouldn't hang her but she'd be old before she could walk free again. It wasn't all Knut's fault—he hadn't forced her to kill Molly—but a good share of it was. A good share of it was.

Chapter 31

There are some cases you leave feeling pretty good about yourself. This wasn't one of them. I don't suppose I liked Emma much or approved of what she'd done but the sadness I felt was for her. I think she'd probably been a pretty decent woman till Knut twisted her all up inside.

Emma was going to a prison with walls and bars.

But Knut was going to a prison, too. He'd never forgive himself. And that was as it should be.

I was thinking all this as I walked to Liz's house for supper. I was hoping to get her drunk enough to forget my so-called advanced age.

A fool never gives up hope, does he?